Something isn't right her lid of her box and hesita

"Come on, Jess," said Hunter. His voice sounded strange through the werewolf mask—deeper and huskier. "Get dressed and let's go!"

She stared at the box, then sighed and lifted the lid. She grabbed the green-skinned witch mask and took it out. It was heavy, like lifting a severed head. She stared at the haggard, wart-riddled face with the long, wiry black hair. Jessie brought it over her head and pulled it into place. She was shocked to find that the inside of the mask was warm and moist. As she unfolded the pointed black hat and unfurled the tattered black cloak, the mask seemed to tighten around her head like something hungry and alive.

Her vision swam for a moment, then cleared. The mask stopped its constriction and actually felt comfortable now. She finished dressing and looked down at her hands. They were bony and putrid green in color. Her fingernails were no longer short and bitten to the quick. They were long and jagged and jet black in color...

THE HALLOWEEN STORE

& AND OTHER TALES OF ALL HALLOWS' EVE

BY RONALD KELLY

DEDICATION

For Tosha Gulley and Marie Kirkland... lovers of horror, of vampires, of Halloween. 24/7... 365.

CONTENTS

INTRODUCTION

I'd been thinking about doing another Halloween collection for a while now, since *Mister Glow-Bones & Other Halloween Tales* was released back in 2015. Of course, the year I finally decided to do it would have to be 2020.

What a chaotic shitstorm of a year it's been so far. The ebb and flow of the dreaded COVID-19, folks wearing masks and social distancing (and fighting about it), civil unrest, Black Lives Matter versus law enforcement, buildings burning, national monuments graffitied, statues defaced and torn down, the worse political party rivalry in the nation's history, the murder hornets that never showed up. Then there was the terrifying Zombie/Alien Battle of Pensacola Beach (What? You missed that one?).

Take it from me—and I've been around a few decades—but I ain't ever seen anything like 2020 come around the pike... sort of like a flaming runaway semi-truck full of angry Tasmanian devils, red waspers, and homicidal clowns.

So, let's think about Halloween for a moment. A 2020 Halloween. It's bound to be a helluva lot different from all the other Halloweens we've had before. Will kids wear masks beneath their masks? Will costumes be anti-viral instead of flame-retardant? Will you have to leave a big bowl of candy or treat bags on the front porch and wave to the Trick-or-Treaters through the window? Will there even be any toilet paper to roll yards with this year, or is that too valuable a commodity to waste?

Or, heaven forbid, will there even be a Halloween at all?

To tell the truth, that's a dreadful and depressing notion

to even comprehend. We practically postponed Easter and the Fourth of July. Will Halloween be any different? Will state and county governments decide that our kids are far too valuable to be put at risk and actually outlaw All Hallows' Eve for this October? And what about next year?

I'll tell you what... let's not even think about that here. Consider *The Halloween Store & Other Tales of All Hallows' Eve* as your safe place. Other writers are incorporating COVID and social unrest/injustice into their fiction, but you won't find it here. Why do we want to rehash and elaborate on all those crappy things over and over again, when we can have fun, get the armchair shivers, and feel like kids again?

I have five brand new tales for you within these pages, Halloween versions of a couple of old RK favorites, and two essays about Halloweens past. I'm hoping they'll take your mind off nasty, ol' 2020 for a while. Maybe transport you to simpler, more care-free days when Halloween was just as special and anticipated as Christmas was. When choosing your costume, mapping out your Trick-or-Treat route, and gathering with your siblings and neighborhood friends was an event you looked forward to all year long.

So, sit back and feel the crunch of autumn leaves beneath your sneakers... smell the tangy scent of wood smoke and greasepaint in the air... see the blazing grin of the Jack-O'-Lantern and the eerie glow of the cardboard skeleton dancing to the music of children's laughter and the satisfying thud of Tootsie Rolls, Smarties, and Fun-Size Snickers hitting the bottom of your treat bag.

But first, let's all head down to the Halloween Store...

Ronald Kelly
Brush Creek, Tennessee
August 2020

THE HALLOWEEN STORE

It was the posters that appeared all over town that got them excited.

Stapled to telephone poles, taped to the windows of the beauty parlor and the drugstore, pinned to the bulletin board in the Pikesville post office. Bright DayGlo orange with bold black printing, embellished with creepy images of skulls, black cats, and spider webs, they read:

Come Visit
THE HALLOWEEN STORE!
Spooky, Horrific, Terrifying!
Best Selection in Town!
Masks and Costumes!
Indoor & Outdoor Decorations!
Vintage Halloween Items!
Free Mystery Gift with First Purchase!
203 South Main Street

"I think we oughta head over there right now," Hunter told them. "Take a look at what they have and maybe buy a little something to get that free mystery gift."

The other two boys, Mike and Scott, agreed completely. But of course, for them, everything Hunter said and suggested was like a word from God Himself. Jessie wasn't as convinced. She didn't take their leader's word as gospel nearly as easily as the other two.

"I don't know. We could probably get the same stuff cheaper at Walmart or the Dollar Tree. Those specialty shops can be pretty expensive, you know."

Hunter rolled his eyes. "But then we wouldn't get the mystery gift, would we? Besides, they have vintage stuff. You can't get that at Walmart."

Jessie couldn't argue with that. "Well, I'm kinda short on money," she finally admitted. "I spent all of my allowance last week on a new Pop Socket for my phone and I'm broke."

"I'll loan you a couple of dollars," volunteered Scott.

"Me, too," said Mike. "I've got some left over from last week."

"See?" Hunter told her. "We've got you covered. Now let's head on over and take a look."

"You think they're still open? It's already past 4:30."

Hunter sighed and shook his head. It was an annoying gesture that drove Jessie up the wall sometimes. "Halloween stores don't close early, Jess. Most of their customers are adults and they don't get off from work until five o'clock or so. Probably doesn't even close until eight or nine."

"Well... okay. Let's go then."

The four set their bikes in motion and pedaled down Juniper Avenue, in the direction of West Main. The afternoon air was crisp and cool, and the gutters between the sidewalks and street were thick with autumn leaves. Last year, October had been unseasonably warm throughout the month. But this year it was perfect. Just the way it ought to be.

The Halloween Store was in a little strip mall at the far end of South Main, where the town businesses gave way to churches and neighborhoods, and then into rural countryside, clear to the old bridge that crossed the muddy swell of the Harpeth River. Beyond that, the highway left Mangrum County and crossed over into Fear County... a place folks tended to avoid like the plague for some reason. There were only five businesses in the strip mall: Juan's Mexican Restaurant, the Sun Goddess Tanning Salon, a thrift store called Finders-Keepers, the Double-Dip ice cream shop, and the store they had come to visit.

They parked their bikes out front and stood in front of the store for a long moment. "Well, it certainly doesn't look like the poster made it out to be," Jessie said skeptically.

"Aw, you know what they say." Hunter looked at her like

she was supremely stupid. "You can't judge a book by its cover."

Jessie's ears reddened. Good thing they were hidden beneath her long brown hair. Sometimes Hunter could be a real asshole, as insufferable as her new stepfather, Roger, was. Sometimes she felt she might have a crush on the boy. That, in itself, was confusing and hard to process for a twelve-year-old.

She regarded the storefront. There was nothing to distinguish it as particularly special, just the rental space in the very center of the strip mall, but one that had been unoccupied for seven or eight months, from what she could recall. There was no official sign above it like the other businesses. Its dingy, plate-glass window had been painted in brilliant shades of orange, green, and white—jack-o'-lanterns, ghosts, black cats, flying bats, and the silhouette of a witch on a broom against a full moon. In the middle of it all, ghoulish purple letters proclaimed THE HALLOWEEN STORE. On the door of the shop hung a glow-in-the-dark skeleton. It held a sign that read "We're Open! Come on in... if you DARE!!"

"Well, come on," urged Hunter. He absently ran his fingers through his bright red hair, which was cut short on the sides and back, and was bushy on top, sort of like Kid Flash in the comic books. "Let's see what they got."

He opened the door. A sensor was tripped, and a speaker somewhere let out a bloodcurdling scream. The four jumped, then laughed at themselves as they walked inside.

The store was dim and shadowy. There were fluorescent lights overhead, but they were as dusty as the window was and gave off half the light that they should have. The store had a musky, mildewed odor to it, like damp concrete and mold, or how Jessie's grandmother's potato cellar smelled when she visited her out on her farm. There were several aisles of shelves, each boasting Halloween items like light-up plastic pumpkins, fake spider web, plastic chains, and those big inflatable decorations that folks put in their yards. Along the walls hung Halloween costumes for all ages, like the ones you could get at most retail stores. There were also makeup kits and latex appliances to adhere with spirit gum: bullet holes, scars, and warty witches noses.

They walked down the center aisle, checking out the merchandise. Most of it was stuff they had already seen before, year after year. "See," whispered Jessie. "Twice as high as Walmart."

Hunter turned and gave her a withering glare. "Just give it a chance. There's bound to be some good stuff in here somewhere."

When they reached the back of the store, they came to a long counter. Behind it sat a small, elderly woman. Her hair was an odd shade of silver-blue and her face was plump and cheerful. Black horn-rimmed glasses hung from a golden chain around her neck. She looked as though she should be wearing a church dress, as old as she was, but instead she was decked out in a black t-shirt with THE HALLOWEEN STORE printed across her ample bosom in ghastly green letters. Pinned above the letter H was a name tag that read MISS HAZEL.

"Well, hello, kids!" she greeted enthusiastically. "Welcome to The Halloween Store! Anything particular you're looking for?'

"No," said Hunter. "Just looking."

"Take your time," Miss Hazel said. "We're open till nine, so you have plenty of time."

Hunter turned and eyed Jessie with a smirk. *See... I told you so.*

"Thank you, ma'am," the girl said politely. They stood before the counter and studied what was in the bins in front. Rubber bats and tarantulas, fake eyeballs, and party favors like spider rings, skull pencil erasers, and plates and napkins bearing leering jack-o'-lanterns. There was candy, too. Bags of bite-sized candy bars, candy corn, bubble gum, and suckers.

But it was what was *behind* the counter that drew their attention the most.

A long sign, in red letters dripping blood, read VINTAGE HALLOWEEN ITEMS. There on the shelves and hanging around them were Halloween decorations and costumes that they had never seen or had only seen in old magazines or online on eBay. There were rubber monster masks with fuzzy fake hair, plastic trick-or-treat pumpkins, and cardboard cutouts of black cats, witches, and tombstones to hang on your wall. To one side of the shelves hung a jointed, glow-in-the-dark skeleton in its original packaging. The card on top read: LIFE-SIZED MISTER GLOW-BONES! GLOW-IN-THE DARK! 5 FEET TALL! FULLY ARTICULATED! AMAZE AND TERRIFY YOUR FRIENDS!

"See anything you like?" Miss Hazel asked.

"Uh, yes, ma'am!" said Scott. "All of it, really."

The others nodded in agreement.

"How old is this stuff?" Hunter wanted to know.

"Some it is from the Sixties and Seventies," she replied. "Other stuff is from the Eighties and Nineties. All of it before you were even born."

Jessie's eyes were drawn to a shelf on the wall behind the old woman. Four boxes stood side by side: colorfully printed cardboard with cellophane windows in the center of the top lid. REAL MONSTERS! they read, DELUXE HALLOWEEN COSTUMES. From the clear windows leered the masks of the monsters inside: a werewolf, a vampire, a witch, and an Egyptian mummy.

"Those are kind of cool," she said.

The woman glanced over her shoulder and smiled. "Yes... and they're rare, too. That costume company wasn't around very long. One Halloween season, in fact. Then they went out of business."

Hunter stepped forward and studied the costume boxes. The masks inside weren't those thin-shelled, cheaply painted masks with the elastic bands that were common in the old Ben Cooper boxed sets. These were extremely detailed. Every wrinkle, every scar, every wart and blemish seemed to stand out in disturbing relief, as though the masks were made of actual flesh. Even the teeth were yellow and jaggedly sharp, like actual bone, instead of painted plastic.

"I suppose those are pretty pricey, aren't they?"

"Only twenty dollars each," said Miss Hazel. "But, for you kids, I can knock it down to eighteen."

The kids were surprised at how reasonable the price was. "Well, we don't have that much right now..." began Jessie.

"... but we can get it!" Hunter added quickly. "A couple of weeks of allowance money ought to do it."

Miss Hazel grinned. There was something about that smile

that bothered Jessie. It took her a moment and then she remembered. A Little Golden Book of Hansel and Gretel her mother read to her when she was little. The old witch that trapped the brother and sister in the gingerbread house had grinned like that—mischievously, hungrily, as she fattened the pair up for the oven.

"From what I figure, there's exactly two weeks until Halloween," Miss Hazel told them. "If you four really, really want them, I'll be happy to put them away for you."

"Sure!" said Hunter. "No problem. We could do that!"

Jessie nudged the boy in the ribs and whispered out of the side of her mouth. "Hey! I'm not sure I can save that much in two weeks."

"We'll make it happen," he whispered back.

"Fine." Miss Hazel stretched up on tippy-toes and gathered each of the costume boxes. They expected the shelf to be empty afterwards, but there seemed to be another box lying flat on the shelf, behind where the others had stood.

"Hey, what's that one?" asked Scott.

Miss Hazel glanced back up at the shelf. "Oh, that one's already taken, I'm afraid."

They tried to read the printing on the end of the box, but between the shadows within the far reaches of the shelf and the dust that covered the cardboard, they couldn't quite make it out.

"So... who's going to get what?" the storeowner asked them.

"I want the werewolf!" blurted Hunter before anyone else could.

"The vampire," said Mike.

"And I'll have the mummy," Scott told her.

Jessie shrugged her narrow shoulders. "I guess I'll take the witch then."

"Wonderful!" The old lady stacked the costume boxes one upon the other, then stashed them beneath the counter, out of sight.

"If we buy a little something, do we still get the mystery gift?" Hunter asked.

"Of course," said Miss Hazel. "I'll tell you what... since

you're buying the costumes, I'll just go ahead and give the mystery gifts to you now. How does that sound?"

"That sounds terrific!" said Scott. The others nodded in agreement.

Miss Hazel reached into a drawer behind the sales counter and brought out four squares wrapped in shiny gold foil. Stamped on the front of each was a leering jack-o'-lantern and the words HAPPY HALLOWEEN.

"Thanks, Miss Hazel!" Hunter grabbed one off the counter. The other three followed and soon had their mystery gift in hand.

"Well, I guess we'd better be getting home to supper," Jessie said.

"Thanks for dropping by, kids," said the elderly woman. "Remember, you'll need to pay for these costumes by October thirty-first or they go back on the shelf."

"Yes, ma'am," Hunter assured her. "We'll have the money by then."

The four left The Halloween Store and ran to their bikes. Before they left, they looked at one another and quickly tore the foil from their mystery gifts.

Each held a trading card, bearing the holographic image of a particular monster.

"Weird," said Hunter. "I got a werewolf. The same as my costume." He turned the card in the fading light of late afternoon. The image of a man on the card began to contort and sprout fur, until he finally changed into a snarling lycanthrope.

The other three marveled at their own prizes. Gracing the cards were uncannily realistic images of a vampire, a mummy, and a witch. Each were identical to the costumes they had picked out.

"Big coincidence, huh?" Mike said with a grin. The mummy on his card crept from an ancient sarcophagus and shambled forward, bony arms outstretched.

Yeah, right, thought Jessie. *She knew which ones she was giving us.*

The courthouse clock rang the hour of five several blocks away.

"Crap!" said Hunter. "I'm late for supper!"

"Me, too!" Jessie added. "My mom's gonna have my hide!"

The four tucked their trading cards away in their jacket pockets, hopped on their bikes, and pedaled swiftly back down the street for home.

Several days before Halloween, they met at the Dairy Queen to pool their resources.

Hunter finished counting out the dollar bills and change they had deposited in the middle of the table. "We've got sixty-eight dollars and eleven cents. I figure with sales tax, we need a grand total of seventy-nine bucks. So, we're eleven short."

They all looked at Jessie. She was the one who had brought the least to the pile.

"You know I don't get as much allowance as you do," she told them, embarrassed. "My stepdad is an asshole and cheap as crap." That wasn't all he was, but she didn't care to elaborate. "I've got a babysitting gig on Thursday night. That'll give me eight more."

"Maybe we can pick up aluminum cans tomorrow afternoon and sell them to Old Ben at the junkyard to make up the rest," suggested Scott.

"We can't screw this up," Hunter told them firmly. "If we do, goodbye costumes. We'll end up going as ourselves on Halloween and what fun is that gonna be?"

They grew silent in the booth at the rear of the restaurant. Jessie idly took her witch card from her pocket and turned it back and forth, watching the holographic image move. The old hag stirred a boiling cauldron as a black cat leapt onto her shoulder and hissed.

"Do you ever wonder if there really are... you know... *monsters*?" she asked after a moment.

Hunter snorted through his nose. "Are you serious?"

"The legends and stories. Bigfoot, the Loch Ness Monster, the Mothman... they've got to have some basis in fact, don't they?"

Their leader shook his head. "It's just folklore and crap like that. Scary stories to tell over a campfire."

Mike spoke up. "They say there was a monster here in Mangrum County once."

Jessie felt goosebumps prickle her arms. "You mean the Snake-Critter?"

"Yeah. That thing that killed all those farm animals way back in the 1940s. They say it stole kids, too. Took them to a cave and fed upon them."

"That's bullshit!" Hunter laughed. "You actually believe that old story?"

"Maybe it's true," Scott suggested. "My grandfather knows Old Man Sweeny. He was a kid back then. Said the Snake-Critter took his prized hog and drug it across a pasture."

"Yeah, and I've heard he claims that he and his daddy and an old black man hiked into Fear County to find a way to defeat it," Hunter said. "Just tall tales and lies. You know as well as I do, nobody goes to Fear County unless they have a damn good reason. Besides, Old Man Sweeny is in his eighties. He's a step or two away from Alzheimer's. Might even have it already."

"I've heard other stories, too," Jessie told them. "About weird things going on all over Tennessee. That creature called the Dark'Un, that can change its form... and that coven of were-wolves in Old Hickory. And an old mountain preacher who was turned into a vampire."

"Like I said, bullshit... all of it." Hunter looked at his friends and shook his head. "Stop acting like a bunch of four-year-olds pissing your panties. Let's stick to Halloween and whether we're going to score those vintage costumes or not."

The others nodded and grew silent.

Smug jackass! thought Jessie. She ignored Hunter and turned the hologram card around in her fingers, watching the witch stir the boiling contents of the cauldron, while the black cat arched its back and hissed menacingly. Jessie had always considered herself to be a tomboy, which was why she was disappointed when she ended up with the last costume of the four. But since then... since discovering her mystery card was the witch... she had grown rather fond of the old hag. She actually looked forward to donning the ragged black cloak, pointed hat, and the narrow, hawk-nosed mask of putrid green. She even considered sneaking her mom's broom out of the utility room closet to complete the ensemble.

After school let out on October 31st, Jessie and the others biked across town to The Halloween Store.

Hunter took a wad of bills from midway down his left gym sock and slapped it on the counter. "Here you go, Miss Hazel," he said with a big grin on his face. "Paid in full!"

The elderly woman counted the money, nodded in satisfaction, and then pushed their change across the counter... two quarters, a dime, and four pennies.

She reached under the counter and brought out the four boxed costumes. Before she handed them over, however, she reached into a drawer and placed four sheets of paper and an ink pen before them.

"What's this?" asked Scott.

"A disclaimer," she replied. "You'll each need to sign one and date it."

Jessie was surprised. "A disclaimer? For Halloween costumes? How come?"

"It only states that you take responsibility for these items and that The Halloween Store is not liable for the misuse of the contents within," she told the girl politely. "It's only a formality, dear. What happens with these costumes on All Hallows' Eve will become null and void at midnight, when October ends and November begins."

That's ridiculous, Jessie thought, but that wasn't how it felt at all. Instead, the contracts sent up a red flag of alarm. "I don't know about..."

"Aw, just sign it and let's get out of here!" Hunter grabbed the pen and quickly signed his paper. Scott and Mike shrugged and did the same.

Jessie looked at the sheet of paper. *This isn't right.*

"Jessie!" Hunter glared at her impatiently. "It'll be dark before long. We've got to get ready."

"Okay, okay!" The girl grabbed the pen and signed the disclaimer.

They each took their costume box and headed for the door.

"Thanks, Miss Hazel!" Hunter said, his voice nearly drowned out by the bloodcurdling scream as they exited the store.

"Happy Halloween, kids!" called Miss Hazel. "Have fun!"

Jessie was the last one out. Before crossing the sidewalk to her bike, she glanced back. Through the window, Miss Hazel stood behind the counter with that ugly hag grin on her face. As the portal to the store eased shut, it made a clang like the closing of a heavy oven door.

They went home, changed out of their school clothes into their trick-or-treating clothes, and met back at Scott's house as the sun was setting in the west.

They gathered in the back yard and began to hurriedly change into their costumes.

Hunter was dressed in a flannel shirt and blue jeans. He opened his box. Inside was a full-head werewolf mask and wooly, clawed hands. When he lifted the mask, he grinned. "Damn! It feels... *weird.* Like... real flesh."

They watched as he pulled the mask over his head and aligned the eyeholes so he could see. He took the clawed gloves and pulled them on. They fit snuggly, drawing closely to his hands like a second skin.

Mike was next. He took the vampire mask from his box and put it on. The pale, bloodless flesh clung to his face, expressing every frown, twitch, and grimace. As he donned the silky black cape with the high collar, Jessie was startled to see that Mike's eyes had turned blood red in color.

"I guess it's my turn." Scott pulled the mask of the Egyptian mummy over his head. As he did so, they could hear the flesh crackle with dryness and a powdery dust fell from the forehead and bony cheeks. He stepped into the one-piece costume and wiggled into it. As he reached around and fastened the clasp at the back of his neck, the cloth wrappings seemed to meld and become seamless. When he brought his hands back around, they were emaciated and wrinkled. Which was odd, since no mummy gloves had come with his costume box.

Something isn't right here, thought Jessie. She reached for the lid of her box and hesitated.

"Come on, Jess," said Hunter. His voice sounded strange

through the werewolf mask—deeper and huskier. "Get dressed and let's go!"

She stared at the box, then sighed and lifted the lid. She grabbed the green-skinned witch mask and took it out. It was heavy, like lifting a severed head. She stared at the haggard, wart-riddled face with the long, wiry black hair. Jessie brought it over her head and pulled it into place. She was shocked to find that the inside of the mask was warm and moist. As she unfolded the pointed black hat and unfurled the tattered black cloak, the mask seemed to tighten around her head like something hungry and alive. Her vision swam for a moment, then cleared. The mask stopped its constriction and actually felt comfortable now. She finished dressing and looked down at her hands. They were bony and putrid green in color. Her fingernails were no longer short and bitten to the quick. They were long and jagged and jet black in color.

"I... I don't feel so good," muttered Scott. His arms hung stiffly at his sides, looking much thinner than they normally did, as though there were only bones beneath the ancient gauze and nothing more. "I think I'm gonna have to go in and lay down for a while. I'll catch up with you guys later." He doubled over and coughed violently. A dry puff of sandy-brown dust expelled from the hollows of his mouth and nostrils.

Jessie's thoughts were becoming hazy and disjointed. *What's happening? What has she done to us?* A shrill cackle involuntarily escaped her throat. It sounded sinister and brimming with malevolence.

"Ready to go?" Hunter no longer sounded anything like himself. What came out of his mouth was a cross between human words and bestial growling. The fangs of his mask dripped thick streamers of saliva, like a dog that hadn't eaten for several days and was on the point of starvation.

Jessie looked around for Mike. He no longer stood where he was. Something fluttered and flew by her head. She looked up and saw a bat outlined in the pale orb of the full moon. Then it was gone.

Her thoughts slowly cleared and, abruptly, she understood. "Yes, I'm ready."

Together, the werewolf and the witch entered the gathering gloom, one heading for State Street, while the other disappeared in the direction of Walnut Avenue.

Later that evening, Elaine and Roger Blackwell, Jessie's mother and stepfather, were called to the sheriff's office. They were surprised when the law officer met them at the front desk. His face was pale and shaken. He looked as though he was having a very rough night. Something was going on, that was for sure. The office was a hive of frantic activity.

"What's going on, Frank?" Roger asked him.

"Where's Jessie?" Elaine demanded. Her narrow face was full of concern and worry.

"I'll take you to her in a minute," Sheriff Winfree assured her. "First, let's step into my office and talk."

Soon, the sheriff was behind his desk, while Roger and Elaine sat in chairs facing him.

Frank Winfree lifted his coffee mug to his lips and took a long sip. His hand trembled, causing the beverage to spill onto his desk blotter.

"Okay," he finally said. "Your daughter has three friends she hangs around with—Hunter Brown, Scott McGill, and Mike Preston."

"Yes," agreed Elaine.

"Well, believe it or not, they've caused quite a bit of havoc in Pikesville tonight."

Roger laughed. "What do you mean *havoc*? Rolling people's yards? Egging car windshields?"

Sheriff Winfree looked as though he were at the end of his rope. "I wish to God that was the extent of it." He paused and took another sip of coffee, then continued. "Do you know Nick Dandridge?"

"Sure," said Elaine. "Tom and Betty Dandridge's boy. Jessie and her friends have had trouble with him at school. He's sort of a... bully."

"Not anymore. He's dead. We have a dozen witnesses that claim Hunter Brown attacked him and tore his throat clean out. With his teeth."

"You've got to be kidding," said Roger.

They could tell by his expression that he wasn't. "The boy is dressed up in a werewolf costume that doesn't *look* like a costume at all. He's locked up in a cell right now. And he's *bent* a couple of the bars, trying to get out. I've got a deputy down there with a shotgun, in case he does."

Roger and Elaine looked at him like he was crazy.

The lawman continued. "Mike Preston. Dressed like a vampire. At five-thirty-five, he was seen walking, hand in hand, with the Andersons' six-year-old daughter, Heather. An hour later, she was found lying in a ditch, unconscious and anemic. Heather died at the hospital at seven-fifteen." The sheriff paused for a moment to compose himself. "At seven-forty-two, she was seen leaving through the emergency room doors. An orderly ran to stop her, but she was gone. A couple of bats dive-bombed him, then flew off into the night."

"What about Jessie?" Elaine wanted to know. Her face was pale and sickly.

"I'll come to her in a moment," said Winfree. "First... Scott McGill. His parents claimed he came back into the house after he dressed in his Halloween costume... a mummy, they said. He told them he wasn't feeling well, then went into his room and shut the door. After a half hour, they grew concerned. They found him stretched out on his bed with his arms folded across his chest. They said it didn't look like their son at all... more like something out of a museum. Said his room smelled musky, like a tomb. Joe McGill reached down to wake Scott up and... and... he kind of *crumbled*. Just fell apart... like he was all dried up."

"That's crazy, Frank," Roger said. "All of it. So, where's our daughter right now?"

"She's locked in an interrogation room down the hall."

"Jessie?" Elaine was shocked and indignant. "What could my sweet, innocent daughter have done to deserve..."

"More than you could imagine," Winfree told her. "She's dressed up like a witch. Black hat and cloak, ugly green face, the whole nine yards. And, believe it or not, she's been doing what witches are known to do."

Roger laughed, but the sound was full of contempt rather than humor. "Like what? Hexes and spells? Conjuring?"

"You said it, not me," the sheriff replied. "There's a group of girls from her school... cheerleaders... who have been making fun of her, from what I've been told. Terri Stapleton and a few others." The man stopped and stared down at his hands, frowning, as if wrestling with what he had seen with his own eyes. "They're... they're *trees* now."

"Trees? What the hell do you mean... *trees?*"

Frank Winfree looked up, his eyes wild. "Just what I said, Roger! She turned them into freaking trees! Oak, maple, sycamore, magnolia! Rooted into the asphalt in the middle of Dexter Avenue. You can see their faces carved in the trunks... horrified, screaming!"

Frightened, Elaine began to cry. Roger's face was red with anger. "That's bullshit! I'm not going to stand here and..."

"Then let's go ask her ourselves," Winfree said, standing up. "Sally Watson is keeping an eye on her. I thought it best to have a female deputy stay in the room with her. She seemed a little hostile toward the male officers."

Together, they left the sheriff's office and walked down the hall to a door at the very end. Winfree unlocked it and led the way in.

In the center of the room was a single table. Jessie sat there, dressed in her witch costume, her thin green hands folded one atop the other. She stared at them as they came through the door and grinned with yellowed, rotten teeth.

"Hi, Mom!" The grin faded when she saw the man standing next to her mother. "Roger."

"Has she been behaving herself, Sally?" the sheriff asked as he closed the door.

Deputy Watson simply sat in the corner, silently, unwilling to answer... or unable to.

The sheriff's stomach sank. Slowly, he walked over and reached out... touched the woman's face... and discovered that it was as hard as stone.

"I don't like people staring at me," Jessie told him. "And that's all she did... just sat there and stared at me... like she was a statue or something." She grinned that ugly picket-fence grin. "So, I made her into one."

"This is idiotic!" Roger raged. His angry eyes fastened on his stepdaughter. "Jessie, you take that damn mask off *right now!*" When she made no effort to do so, he started across the room to do it for her.

The girl raised her wrinkled, green hand and said *"Hush!"*

Immediately, Roger Blackwell stopped in his tracks. His face grew dark purple in hue and his eyes bulged from their sockets. He dropped to his knees and began to puke. But it wasn't his dinner of roast beef and mashed potatoes that rose from his throat. Instead, a gorge of tar-black liquid erupted from his open mouth. As it struck the concrete floor of the interrogation room, they could see things in the dark vomit, wiggling and crawling. Worms, spiders, maggots, and scorpions.

"Jessie!" screamed her mother, terrified.

"No, Mom," Jessie said, her jaundiced eyes full of fury. "He deserves it. Haven't you noticed how he looks at me? I'm not even a teenager yet and he looks at me like he wants to… wants to sneak into my room and…!" Contemptuously, she clenched her fist. A few feet away, Roger moaned and gagged as a long, black snake worked its way past his lips and coiled upon the floor, thrashing and hissing.

Elaine looked shocked. "Roger?"

The big man attempted to rise to his feet. "She's lying, Elaine! The little bitch is…"

"Shut up, freak!" shrieked Jessie. She flipped her hand and recited words from a dialect they had never heard before. A crushing force bore down on Roger, slamming him violently to the floor. His nose exploded and most of the bones of his face fractured as his head met the concrete with a hollow thud. Blood spurted in a dozen directions, mingling with the inky contents of his stomach.

She looked over at Frank Winfree. He was standing there with his hand resting on the butt of his service revolver. "What do you intend to do with that, Sheriff? Shoot a twelve-year-old girl?"

Frightened, Winfree slowly eased his hand away from the gun.

"Like I told you before, it'll all be over with come midnight," she told him. "The lady who sold us the costumes said so."

"The lady at The Halloween Store?" clarified the law officer. He looked over at Deputy Watson in the corner. Her face and hands were as gray as granite now, and so were her eyes.

"Sure, go ask her yourself. She might still be there... if you hurry."

Sheriff Winfree gently eased Elaine Blackwell toward the door. He bent down and, with some effort, helped Roger to his feet. Her stepfather stared at her, dumbfounded, his battered face covered with blood and nasty black barf.

Jessie cackled shrilly, causing them to move a little faster. Her fiery gaze was centered on her mother's husband. "Get the hell outta here, pervert!"

When the door had slammed behind them and the rattle of the lock engaging sounded, Jessie sat there and laughed to herself. She glanced over at the still form in the chair across the room. "Nothing to say, Deputy Watson?"

Tiny cracks and fissures began to creep across the police-woman's cheeks and the knuckles of her hands.

There was a clock hanging on the wall above the interrogation room door. The hands showed the time as 8:39.

"So much to do, so little time," Jessie mused. "Double, double, toil and trouble, and all that neat stuff." The thought struck her as funny and she cackled long and loud with wicked glee.

The girl left her chair and walked to the cinderblock wall opposite from the door. Raising her arms, her eyes lost their yellow cast and turned coal black, like shiny marbles of polished ebony.

As she chanted an ancient incantation, the mortar between the blocks began to glow and slowly melt away.

Sheriff Winfree found the door to The Halloween Store locked. Peering through the glass, he found the interior to be pitch dark.

He took the long, black flashlight from his gun belt and shattered the glass, then carefully reached through and disengaged the deadbolt.

Behind him—from his patrol car radio—echoed a half-dozen

radio calls. It sounded as though his deputies had their hands full.

The lawman opened the door and turned on his light. The store was empty. No merchandise, no shelves... nothing at all. As he walked farther into the shop, he focused the beam of the flashlight ahead. All he saw was bare, concrete floor... until he reached the very center.

The circle of pale-yellow light settled on a single object. An open box. One section was the bottom, while the other was a lid with a cellophane window in its center.

He walked forward and directed the beam into the box.

Only two objects were inside. A pair of black, horn-rimmed glasses on a golden chain... and a name tag that read MISS HAZEL.

He hooked the toe of his shoe beneath the lid of the box and flipped it over. Emblazoned across the cardboard were five words in stark, blood red.

HOMICIDAL MANIAC SUPER DELUXE COSTUME.

"Car 14 requesting backup!" came the voice of Deputy Saunders from the patrol car's radio. "We've got a Code 217 in progress! Repeat... Code 217!" A tense pause, then Saunders' voice grew frantic. "Ma'am... put down the knife! Put down the knife down now or I'll be forced to..."

Frank Winfree held his breath and waited for his deputy's scream. It came a moment later, long and loud, full of agony and terror.

"Dammit!" groaned the sheriff, running for the door. "Is this night ever going to end?"

The courthouse clock rang the hour of nine on the other side of town.

Three more hours of Halloween to go.

Winfree prayed for midnight but knew that it would be a long time coming.

MISTER MACK
IS BACK IN TOWN

His heart jumped when his cell phone rang.

Oh God... please, let this be good news.

It was his wife, Gloria.

"They found her!"

Kyle Sadler didn't know whether to be relieved or scared half to death. He and half the town had been looking for his ten-year-old daughter, Rebecca, most of the night. She and her best friend, Hannah, had started home from school the previous afternoon. The walk was short—only a couple of blocks—but they had never arrived home.

His heart hammered in his chest as he asked the question. "Is she... is she alright?"

Gloria was crying, but it was happy tears. "She's *alive*, Kyle. Barely conscious but alive."

Kyle pulled to the side of the road, unsure of how to proceed until he knew exactly what was going on. "What do you mean 'barely conscious'? What's happened to her?"

"They don't know yet. The police called and said EMTs were transporting her to the hospital. Can you swing by and pick me up, and we'll go over there together?"

He put the pickup truck in gear and made a U-turn in the street, heading back the way he had come. "Where did they find her?"

"That's the strange thing. They found her lying in the weeds at the old Bel-Air Drive-In theater out on Highway 51."

"That's way on the other side of town!"

"I know. I don't understand it." Gloria sobbed, but there was something disturbing about the sound this time. "Kyle, the t-shirt she was wearing was turned inside out and her sneakers were on the wrong feet. Oh Lord! Kyle... they think someone undressed her and then put her clothes back on her." Gloria's fears mirrored his own. "You don't think that someone abducted her and..."

Kyle didn't want to think about it. "What about Hannah?"

"They didn't find her," she told him. "She's still missing."

An odd sense of déjà vu passed through Kyle's mind, but he wasn't sure why.

He ran a stop sign and nearly got broadsided. "Honey, I'm almost there. Meet me in the driveway."

A moment later, he saw his wife standing at the foot of the drive, with her purse slung over her shoulder. Her face held the same awful expression of anxiety and fear that his did.

Please, God, he prayed as he braked to a halt and watched Gloria run around the front of the truck to the passenger door. *Let my little girl be okay.*

They arrived at the hospital at the same time the paramedics did.

Kyle parked the truck and he and his wife ran across the parking lot. They reached the emergency room entrance just as they were wheeling her through the pneumatic double-doors.

"Becky, Mama's here." His wife walked along one side of the gurney, while he took the other.

"I'm here, too, baby." Kyle looked down at his daughter and his heart sank. Her face was as pale as a garden slug and her eyelids and lips were blue. He took her small hand in his. It was disturbingly cold to the touch.

Becky's eyes opened. Her gaze was unfocused, almost like she had been drugged. "Daddy?"

"What is it, Beck?" He squeezed her fingers gently, letting her know he was by her side.

"Daddy... he had... he had..."

"I'm listening, sweetheart..."

A strange little smile crossed her pretty face. "He had... a monster mobile."

At that instant, Kyle Sadler felt as though ice water was running through his veins.

"Are you the girl's parents?"

Kyle and Gloria turned to see a young doctor walking toward them, her face concerned and inquisitive. Her honey-blond hair was pinned up into a French braid and she wore round-lensed eyeglasses. Her name tag identified her as Heidi Malkiewicz.

"Yes," replied Gloria. "Kyle and Gloria Sadler. And this is our Becky... Rebecca."

"I know you want to be with her right now, but I need for you to wait out here until we've made our examination and see what's going on. We'll call you just as soon..."

"Check her blood platelets," Kyle told her. "She's terribly anemic. Her white cell count will be dangerously low. Her torso and abdomen will be tender, slightly distended. And run CAT and PET scans."

She stared at him in confusion. "Are you a physician, Mr. Sadler?"

"No," Kyle admitted. "I'm a contractor. Construction and excavation."

"Then how do you know...?"

"I just *do!*" he snapped. He fought down his fear and frustration and lowered his voice. "Please, just check those things, okay?"

Dr. Malkiewicz nodded. "We will." She regarded him strangely, almost suspiciously. "Exactly what do you expect me to find, Mr. Sadler?"

"You'll know when you see it. Or *don't* see it."

A moment later, the two first-responders had wheeled their daughter into the examination area, with Dr. Malkiewicz by her side.

Standing there alone, on the opposite side of those restrictive doors, father and mother stared at one another. Then Gloria fell into Kyle's arms and broke down. He held her close and whispered in her ear. "She'll be okay. I promise."

But would she? He thought of how pale and cold his daughter had been. Not because she had laid in the abandoned lot for an entire October night, but because what was going on inside her was creating that distressing condition.

He also feared for Becky's best friend, Hannah Spaulding, and wondered exactly where she was at that moment.

He had gone there with his best friend, Jimmy Johnson, because they both loved monster movies so much... gone to the big Winnebago camper parked behind an abandoned factory in the industrial park.

They had seen it all. The face and hands of the Creature from the Black Lagoon... Leatherface's patchwork mask from The Texas Chainsaw Massacre... Norman Bates' gray wig, dress, and butcher knife from Psycho... Bela Lugosi's Dracula cape. Dozens of other iconic horror movie props, as well as photos of Mister Mack with Boris Karloff, Lon Chaney Jr., and Vincent Price.

But something about it all bothered Kyle. In the back of his mind, it just didn't add up.

In fact, that place had suddenly felt more like a trap than a museum on wheels.

"This guy is a big fake," Kyle whispered, not wanting the old man to overhear their conversation. "I don't think he worked with any of them. And I think he's lying about being a makeup artist. I've read tons of books on the subject and never once came across anyone named Mack."

"But what about all these cool props? They're for real, aren't they?"

"I doubt it," said Kyle. "Oh, they're elaborate fakes, but I don't think they're the real props. And those photos of him and Karloff and Lugosi... well, you can trick up any kind of photo with a computer these days."

Jimmy shook his head in disgust. "Okay, okay! We'll go. But, if you ask me, you're just being paranoid."

Abruptly the rustle of curtains drew their attention. They turned and gasped.

Behind them, dressed in khaki pants and a Hawaiian shirt—black with orange Halloween jack-o'-lanterns—was a hideous monster.

At least his head was that of some horrid creature. The tanned arms and legs were still those of their elderly host, Mister Mack. Kyle stared, startled, at the monster's face. The skin was a glossy charcoal gray in color with knotty black veins running throughout, like the exposed roots of a tree. The eyes were bulbous and moist, yellow with a network of bulging purple veins and shiny green pupils. It was the teeth that caused his heart to race the most, though. They were small and black, but wickedly jagged and as sharp as razor blades.

Kyle had seen hundreds of horror movies, but never had he seen a creature that looked so damned real.

"Man, you gave us a start!" said Jimmy, finally catching his breath. "That mask just about made me crap in my britches!"

Mister Mack chuckled. It came out as a soft, wet, bubbling noise.

Slowly, Kyle began to back toward the front of the bus.

"Don't tell me that you're still spooked!" laughed Jimmy. He turned back to the man in the Hawaiian shirt. "Great mask, Mister Mack. But how did you make it? You haven't lost your touch. I really like how you make the veins throb like that."

Mister Mack said nothing. He simply started forward... grinning.... with those jagged, black teeth.

"Let's get out of here!" urged Kyle. He suddenly smelled a strange odor in the air of the bus. A stench sort of like the marigolds his mother had planted this past summer.

"What?" Jimmy seemed disoriented, as he stared at his pal. "What's that terrible stink?"

"It's coming from him!" Kyle told him.

Jimmy began to follow his friend, but his face grew strangely pale and he began to gasp for breath. "I... I don't feel right," he said. "My legs..." He collapsed under his own weight. "They... they aren't working."

Kyle tried his best to reach the curtained partition at the front of the bus, but he too was beginning to feel weak and out of kilter. His nasal passages began to sting and his tongue grew numb. "What's happening?" he muttered thickly, then fell into the aisle between the display cases. His arms and legs began to twitch and convulse involuntarily.

Mister Mack started toward them, tiny teeth grating one against the other.

The boy lay on his back staring at the recessed lighting of the *ceiling. Then there he was. Mister Mack… or what masqueraded as Mister Mack. He stared at Kyle for a long moment with those bulging yellow eyes. Then he bent downward and, with no effort at all, lifted Kyle into his arms.*

"No," whispered Kyle. "Please."

"Don't worry," he was assured in that wet, guttural voice that had replaced the elderly man's kindly tone. "I won't hurt you. I promise."

Mister Mack turned and, almost tenderly, began to carry him toward the chamber at the back of the bus.

Kyle awakened from his nightmare with a violent start. He had fallen asleep in one of the two chairs by Becky's bed. He had been out all night, searching for his missing daughter, and must have been more exhausted than he realized.

Gloria reached out and took his hand. "Are you okay?"

He smiled and squeezed her fingers. "Yeah. I just dozed off. Long night."

She sat back in her chair and sighed. "The longest."

"What time is it, hon?" Kyle looked over at the hospital bed that Becky laid in. She was hooked up to every monitor imaginable, as well as a respirator that aided with her breathing. She still looked small and frail and terribly pale.

Gloria glanced at her phone. "2:42." They had been in the private room for nearly three hours now.

Kyle stood up. "I'm going to have to step out for a while. I'll be back in an hour or two."

His wife looked alarmed. "You're just going to leave me here alone? What if she wakes up before you get back?"

"She won't," he assured her. "They have her sedated. She'll sleep the rest of the day. Maybe all night."

"But what's so important that you have to…?"

Kyle Sadler knelt before his wife and took her hands in his. "Gloria… sweetheart… do you remember that story I told you… right after we got married. About when I was in the hospital for a month… when I was twelve?"

Gloria stared at him, uncomprehending at first. Then her eyes widened. "Oh, Kyle… you mean… that man with the camper?"

He was no man, Kyle thought to himself, but didn't tell her that. "Yes."

"You don't think... that *he*...?"

"I don't know," he said calmly. "But I aim to find out. Just sit tight for a while. I'll be back before four-thirty or five."

Gloria nodded. "Okay." As he released her hands, she reached out and laid one on his chest... let it trail past his sternum to his abdomen, until she felt *it*. "Kyle, is Becky... is she going to be like... *you*?"

He said nothing more. He simply kissed her on the forehead and stood up. Then he turned and left the hospital room, heading for the elevator at the end of the corridor.

Kyle walked into the pediatrician's office and looked around. The waiting room was decorated with Sesame Street and Disney characters. Chairs lined the walls, while at the far end was a play area for the kids. There were eight or nine people in the room—moms and dads with their children, waiting to be called.

"May I help you, sir?"

He turned to the woman, a short-haired black lady wearing Rugrats scrubs, at the reception window

"I need to see Dr. Mitchell, please."

She looked past him to see if he had a child with him. "Do you have an appointment?"

"No," he said, knowing this wasn't going to be pleasant. "But it's important that I talk to him. It's about my daughter."

"Is she a patient of Dr. Mitchell's?"

"No, ma'am. But he knows... uh, *knew* me... a long time ago."

"I'm afraid Dr. Mitchell is booked up today, sir," she told him. Her polite voice had taken a harder edge than before. "I can schedule an appointment for your daughter, though, if you'd like."

"My daughter is in the hospital," he said, his voice rising. "She is an extremely sick little girl. Dr. Mitchell can help her. All I need is just a few minutes of his time."

"I'm afraid that's impossible, sir..."

"I don't think you understand!" he said loudly, losing his patience. "This is a matter of life and death, lady!"

Kyle looked past her, into the office beyond. He saw a nurse cut her eyes in his direction, leave her desk, and rush through an adjoining door.

A moment later, a man appeared in the lobby, looking concerned and more than a little inconvenienced. "Yes, sir? I'm Dr. Mitchell. May I help you with something?"

Kyle studied the doctor. It had been a long time ago, but it was definitely the same man. Just as tall, but with a little more weight on him and his hair was thinner and showing a touch of gray.

"I need for you to come with me, Dr. Mitchell," he said. "I have a very sick child."

"I'm afraid I have other patients scheduled, sir. If you'll just get with the receptionist, maybe..."

Kyle's pulse began to quicken... but not in his chest. "Please. You're the only one who can help her. The only one who will *understand!*"

"Mister...?"

"Sadler. Kyle Sadler."

Dr. Mitchell hesitated for a moment. Where had he heard that name before? "Mister Sadler, I must ask you to leave. You're disrupting this office and frightening the children."

Kyle stared at Mitchell and then at the families in the waiting room around him. The adults regarded him with anger and annoyance, while the children were clearly terrified of him and his behavior. He looked over at the receptionist. She picked up a phone and was ready to dial.

Out of desperation, Kyle grabbed the doctor's right hand.

"What the devil are you doing?" snapped Mitchell, attempting to pull away.

Kyle took the man's palm and pressed it against his abdomen, between his sternum and navel.

THRUM, THRUM, THRUM...

Phillip Mitchell's face turned deathly pale.

"Doctor... I'm calling security!" the black woman at the reception window said.

"No." As Kyle released the physician's hand, Dr. Mitchell held up his other hand in dismissal. "No need for that, Miss Anders. I know this man."

"But, Dr. Mitchell..."

"Please have Dr. McKenney take the rest of my appointments this afternoon," he instructed her. Then he regarded the tall man in front of him. "Mr. Sadler... would you please accompany me to my office?"

Kyle followed him as he led the way through the waiting room door and into the suite of examination rooms beyond. At the far end of the corridor was the physician's private office. They entered and Mitchell closed the door behind them.

"Have a seat, Kyle."

Kyle did as he requested. He sat and waited as the doctor took the chair behind the desk.

The doctor sat back and studied him for a long moment. "Damn. This is certainly..."

"Unexpected?"

"A shock is more like it," corrected Mitchell. "How long has it been?"

"Twenty-five years."

The doctor shook his head in wonder. "That long? It seems like it was... yesterday."

Kyle sighed, his eyes regretful. "I'm sorry about what happened out there. It's just... I didn't know who else to turn to."

Mitchell's expression grew concerned. "You said something about a sick child?"

"My daughter... Becky." The pulse in Kyle's abdomen pounded almost painfully. It always did when he grew excited. "Ten years old. Disappeared yesterday afternoon on her way home from school. She was found this morning in a vacant lot... that old drive-in theater on the other side of town...barely conscious, anemic, disoriented."

The concern in the physician's gray eyes turned into alarm. "And they did bloodwork? Other tests?"

"Her white blood cell count was extremely low. They were certain she had leukemia at first. The ultrasound, CAT and PET scans, showed that the position of her organs had been altered."

"The stomach and liver had changed positions," said Mitchell softly, as though peering back in time. "The kidneys were moved to the front of the abdomen. Pancreas missing and, in its place..."

"That pear-shaped organ that has no business being there," said Kyle, finishing his sentence. "Just like mine."

"No sign of sexual assault," the doctor continued. "He's a monster... but not that kind. Maybe something much worse." Phillip Mitchell stood up and walked to the window of his office. Five stories down, the medical center parking lot stretched. It was late in the afternoon, so few vehicles remained. "Was Becky alone?"

"She was when they found her. But her best friend, Hannah, was with her when they left the school grounds. They were excited about working on their Halloween costumes for next week. There was no sign of Hannah at the drive-in. She's still missing."

"Like Jimmy Johnson."

The thought of his childhood friend and the mystery of his whereabouts filled Kyle with sadness. "Yes."

"Did Becky remember what happened?"

"No, she can't recall anything at all. But she did say one thing when we met the paramedics at the hospital."

"And what was that?"

"She said 'Daddy... he had a monster mobile.'"

Dr. Mitchell closed his eyes. "Oh, dear God."

Kyle Sadler knew what the doctor was thinking, because the same thing had been on his mind all day. "He's back."

Phillip stared down at the parking lot for a moment longer. Then he walked to his desk. His cell phone lay next to a framed picture of a pretty middle-aged woman holding two small children... grandchildren, more than likely. The doctor picked up the phone and dialed a number.

When the one on the other end of the line answered, he spoke. "Do you remember the boy in Room 439? Well, he's here, sitting in my office." He waited, while the other talked. "Yes... the bastard is up to his old tricks again. Can we meet? Let's say, seven o'clock... at the Starbucks on Central Street?"

Apparently, the other one agreed.

"Thanks," replied Phillip. "And bring what you have. We'll need it."

After the doctor had ended the call, Kyle stared at him curiously.

"It's someone from back then... when you were a kid," the doctor told him. "You might remember her or might not. We're meeting her later on."

"At seven? And what do we do until then?"

"We'll go to the hospital," Phillip suggested. "I need to see your daughter. We'll tell everyone that I'm her pediatrician. After what's happened to her, I really believe that I ought to be. She'll need someone who understands what has happened to her... someone who has had patients like this before."

"I agree," said Kyle. "Completely."

"Also, the doctors in charge of her case... I'll need to talk to them. Try to explain the physical changes she's gone through... provide access to my files to help them comprehend what they're dealing with."

"What about the police?" asked Kyle. "After Becky was brought in, the doctor told them about what I suggested... about what was wrong with her and what tests she should have. They questioned us pretty hard... suspicious, like they thought we had something to do with it."

"Yeah, I've found that the authorities tend to react like that when it's something strange and unexplainable. I know a man who's still on the force... a detective named Brilson... who investigated your case. I'll talk to him... let him know they're barking up the wrong tree."

As they left the doctor's office and took the elevator downstairs, something bothered Kyle. "You said something... about having *patients*. I thought I was the only one."

Phillip Mitchell turned and looked at him. "Kyle... during the past twenty-five years, I've come across eight children just like you and Becky. Eight who survived what that... that *thing*... did to them. There's no telling how many more there are out there that I don't even know about."

"Oh, God... what is this thing?" muttered Kyle. "What are we up against?"

"I don't know," the pediatrician told him. "I honestly don't. But I believe it's finally time that we deal with it."

After several hours at the hospital, Kyle Sadler and Phillip Mitchell drove across town to the Starbucks on Central Street.

They walked in and looked around. "Over there," directed Phillip. "In that back booth."

When they reached the booth, Kyle was surprised to find an elderly black woman sitting there. She was short with silver hair and a wrinkled face that resembled a road map to a thousand sad and troublesome places. Laying on the table in front of her was a thick, three-ring binder.

"Kyle, this is Sophie Taylor," introduced the doctor. "She was in housekeeping at the hospital when you were there. Do you remember her?"

The contractor studied her smiling face. "Uh, maybe. It was so long ago."

Sophie laughed. Her voice had a husky tone, as though she were a heavy smoker. "Come now, Kyle. Green Lantern and Bit-O-Honey?"

Kyle's eyes widened. "Yes! You brought me something every day. A comic book or candy... something to break the monotony of lying in that bed all day."

Sophie left the booth and embraced him. The elderly woman was so short that her head barely reached the bottom of his chest. She turned her head and laid her ear against his abdomen. A sad smile crossed her dark face.

"It is you. It is my Kyle."

As she moved away, she reached out and gently took one of his big, work-calloused hands... laid it against her own body, just beneath her breastbone.

THRUM, THRUM, THRUM...

Kyle was startled. "You, too?

"Yes," she told him. "In Alabama. 1974. I was nine years old."

"A short, heavyset man... white with a gray beard? Dressed in khakis and a Hawaiian shirt?"

"Yes, but for me it was black. The bastard can do that, you know. Be whatever it wants... because it's all a clever costume. To hide what it really is."

"Why don't we sit down?" suggested Phillip. "We have some serious things to discuss."

The three settled into the booth and looked at one another for a long moment. Then the doctor spoke again. "Sophie has been trying to track him... Mister Mack... for a long time."

The woman nodded. "A *very* long time. Long before you came along, Kyle."

"Just how long has he... *it*... been at this?"

"Who knows. Maybe for decades... maybe centuries. Maybe before the camper it traveled in a chariot or a covered wagon. It has some unknown purpose for the abductions and the alterations... something that benefits it in a very crucial way. It's a predator, but not like a pedophile or a rapist. I believe its needs are essential for its survival."

"Explain the cycles," said Mitchell.

"Cycles?"

"Yes," said Sophie. "I've tracked the abduction and reappearance of missing children in seven states in the past forty years. He seems to do his preying in certain months of the year. January, April, July, and October... one month for each season. I think its body grows weak and depleted during those times and it goes out and hunts for more victims."

"But what the hell does it need from the kids... from *us*? Why does it take what it needs from a few of us and lets us go... but keeps the rest of them? The ones who are never found?" *Like Jimmy... and Hannah.*

"I believe it has something to do with that unknown organ," explained Dr. Mitchell. "The purple, pear-shaped organ. The pancreas is gone, but the mystery organ is left in its place... apparently to serve as a substitute. It's logical to believe that something about the missing organ is what provides this creature with the sustenance it craves... or requires."

Sophie opened her binder. The pages within were like a disturbing and tragic scrapbook. Dozens of articles about abducted and missing children, as well as crayon drawings of Mister Mack, done by children while in the hospital and at home afterward. Kyle caught a glimpse of a newspaper article with his and Jimmy Johnson's face under a headline that read LOCAL

CHILD FOUND, ONE MISSING, FOLLOWING MYSTERIOUS ABDUCTION.

The old woman found what she was looking for. She pulled a map from a plastic sleeve in the middle of the binder and unfolded it, spreading it across the tabletop. "I've logged the patterns of its travel over the past four decades, through Tennessee, Georgia, Alabama, and Mississippi... through Florida, Louisiana, and Texas. It varies its routes enough where you really don't know where he is at any given point in time." A little smile crossed her dark face. "But last month... last month... I finally figured it out."

"Figured *what* out?"

"The creature's base of operation," the doctor told him.

"Its *lair*," clarified the old woman.

"Really? But where—?"

Sophie pressed a stubby, pink-nailed finger on a spot on the map. "Here. Dalton, Georgia."

"The carpet capital of the South?" asked Kyle. "Damn... I make a run down there every other week. Flooring and carpeting is one of the main things we do." He shook his head in disbelief. "I've been going there for nearly six or seven years... and he's been under my nose all along?"

"Yes," said Sophie. "There's an old carpet mill down there... one that got damaged during a tornado and was later abandoned. I went down to the courthouse in Whitfield County a couple of weeks ago and checked the public records. The factory's original owner sold the place thirty-three years ago... to a man named Mack Worthington."

"But it's October," said Kyle. "The thing will be out on the hunt somewhere."

"Yes, it has just begun its autumn cycle," said Sophie. "Your daughter and her friend were the first. But, for some reason, it seems to use the holidays to do the majority of its abductions. New Year's Day, Easter, Fourth of July, Halloween. It's a fair bet that Mister Mack is at that abandoned mill right now... preparing for its next run on the thirty-first."

Kyle sat back in his seat and stared at the binder and the wealth of evidence the elderly woman had compiled. "So, what are we talking about? Capturing him and turning him over to the authorities?"

From the expressions on the faces of Sophie Taylor and Phillip Mitchell, he knew that wasn't what they had in mind at all.

"We can't regard this thing as a *he*, Kyle," Sophie told him. "*It* is a very dangerous and deceptive creature. One that needs to have an end put to it."

"So, we're talking about *killing* it. But... but that would be—"

"Illegal?" mused the doctor. "No. Justified? Yes."

"It isn't a crime to squash an insect or swat a mosquito, is it?" Sophie asked him. "But Mister Mack is neither. It is a monster of some kind. Some mutated form of life... something not from this world."

Kyle couldn't help but laugh. "You mean, an *alien* of some kind?"

"Maybe," the woman agreed. "Or something from the foulest pits of Hell."

Kyle knew that she was right. He thought of his daughter and her friend... and how very frightened they must have been at the moment that Mack's masquerade had ended and it had revealed its true semblance... and nature.

"So, let's hear your plan."

For the next half hour, the three reviewed their options for the extermination of a common menace... a fiend that paraded in the latex skin of a kindly, old man with a roving museum of horror cinema props and lore.

Six days before Halloween, they left town and headed down Interstate 24 toward Chattanooga and the Georgia state line. The three were quiet during the drive, each immersed in their own troubled thoughts. Not only was the idea of actually destroying the thing sobering and disturbing, but their own emotions and reasons for wanting Mister Mack dead set heavily on their minds. Kyle could only guess the motives of his two companions, but his was very clear and concise. He wanted to put an end to the creature for what it had done to him and his daughter... and for what had become of all the unaccounted for... including Jimmy and Hannah.

They reached Dalton around nine-thirty that night. The industrial park on the city's western side was dark, with only a few streetlights here and there. They found the abandoned carpet mill easily, with the help of the GPS in Phillip Mitchell's Lexus. The big building seemed dark and deserted.

As they entered the open gates and circled the factory, Kyle stared into the gloom. "Do you think it's here?"

The car's headlights answered him a moment later. They illuminated a large RV bus—a big forty-five-foot Tiffin motorhome. The thing was huge, painted black with burgundy and silver stripes sweeping majestically down its sides to its nose.

Sophie and Kyle looked at one another. It was an upgraded version of the campers they themselves had fallen victim to. Both knew what was inside, too—Mister Mack's faux collection of horror movie memorabilia. The tantalizing bait at the end of a nasty hook.

"Damn," said Phillip. "That thing must have cost half a million. Where does he get his money?"

"Something that can survive and prey on the innocent as long as it has must have the means to acquire such things," Sophie said. "These days, we're all familiar with predators who are millionaires... even billionaires."

"Yes," said Kyle. What she said was undoubtedly the truth, no matter how disturbing that might be.

They drove around the old building twice, but it appeared to be dark and unoccupied. Finally, the doctor parked the Lexus near the mill's front entrance. The windows were empty of glass and the door stood partially open.

Phillip cut the engine and they sat there for a moment. "Well, here we are," was all he said.

"Yes," said Sophie. "Let's get to it." She was the first to leave the car. She shouldered a large bag and stood staring at the metal front of the old building. The bag looked bulky and uncomfortably heavy. Kyle wondered exactly what she had inside.

The two men met at the trunk. Phillip quietly opened it with the Lexus's key fob. The doctor reached in and took out two shotguns. He handed Kyle a Mossberg 12-gauge pump, while taking a Remington 1100 semi-automatic for himself. Kyle remembered the way Mack had looked without its latex mask. Charcoal gray and glistening, with throbbing veins the size of tree roots. He had no idea what the thing was made of, or how strong or thick its skin might be. It probably wasn't bulletproof... but that wasn't entirely out of the question.

"Miss Sophie," the doctor said quietly. He held out a Browning 9mm pistol to the old woman.

"No, thank you," she declined with a whisper. "I have what I need."

Phillip and Kyle looked at one another. The doctor shrugged and stuck the handgun into the waistband of his pants.

"Here," said Kyle. He opened a plastic toolbox he had brought and removed three respirator masks. He handed one to Mitchell, one to Sophie, and kept one for himself. "We use them when we paint or sandblast. Hopefully, they'll block out those fumes that the thing emits. That paralyzing gas that smells like..."

"Marigolds," answered Sophie.

They slipped the masks over their heads and positioned them beneath their chins, where they would be easily accessible.

Solemnly, the three walked toward the dark building.

When they reached the entrance, Kyle pulled a LED flashlight from his pocket and directed the beam through the doorway. There was a front office, followed by a steel door leading into the belly of the factory. They approached the door and stood there for a moment, listening. They could hear sounds echoing from the other side. A steady dripping, the scurrying of rats amid debris, and something else: the roar of a portable generator and a low, monotonous humming.

"Okay," said the doctor. "Let's go."

They opened the door and went in. The interior of the mill was enormous. The walls seemed to extend up twenty or thirty feet, so high that only darkness could be seen above the heavy steel supports. The workstations and machinery used for manufacturing carpet were still in place—cold, neglected, and riddled with rust.

Despite the building's lack of electricity, there was a brilliant blue glow at the far reaches of the mill. They picked their way through the clutter and finally discovered the source of the illumination.

The generator—a huge, gas-powered, 9375-watt Champion—ran steadily, supplying power to the inexplicable phenomena that they laid witness to.

Every six feet there were strange, metal pods upon the concrete floor, each a good five feet in diameter. From the base of the pods, a broad beam of bright blue energy was emitted, rising vertically to a domed cap that was suspended seven feet overhead. From their count there were two dozen shafts of energy in all.

True, the nature of the technology was beyond their comprehension... as though from another time or place, but it wasn't that which disturbed them the most. It was the things suspended within the energy shafts that both fascinated and horrified them.

Children hung, limp and unresponsive, amid the blue beams, their feet a good two feet off the ground. Girls and boys, from the ages of seven to thirteen. Some of them wore modern clothing, while others wore clothing related to other periods of time: tie-dye shirts and bell bottom pants, cuffed jeans and denim jackets, frilly dresses with button-up shoes.

"Oh God," gasped the pediatrician. "What the hell is this?"

"It's what you beings might call 'suspended animation,'" someone answered from behind. "Isn't that what you call it in your foolish science fiction books? Such a primitive description of an advanced energy dispersement that is beyond your feeble comprehension."

Startled, they turned, expecting to find Mister Mack. But it wasn't him at all... or not the version that they anticipated.

It was a lovely woman in her mid-thirties with long, honey-blond hair, standing a hundred feet away. She wore a pink and black checked flannel shirt, skinny jeans, and a navy-blue windbreaker.

"What do you think?" it asked. "It's new. Children don't trust kindly, geriatric gentlemen any longer. There is too much information about child molesters and sex offenders on social media these days. The youth of today would rather trust a pretty, young Sunday school teacher or soccer mom. So, I adapt with the times and become what is comforting and popular. Go with the flow, as you say."

"Mister Mack," said the contractor.

"Miss Maxine to you, Kyle." The thing laughed when the man seemed alarmed. "Yes, I know you. I know all of my children. What I took from you is a part of me now... and always will be."

"And exactly what is it that you take?" asked Phillip.

"A vital enzyme, Doctor," said Maxine. "One that I can only find in beings of their tender age." It nodded its pretty head toward the suspended children. "I can only retrieve it by syphoning it from the organ you call a pancreas. But, unfortunately, once that enzyme is drained, the organ is utterly useless. That is why I replace it with a duplicate that performs the same function."

Kyle glanced back at the children. He was both relieved and shocked to see his daughter's best friend, Hannah, hanging in the shaft of the fourth beam. Her eyes were open, but glazed and unresponsive. He watched closely and detected the rise and fall of her chest.

"And what about those you keep?" he asked the creature.

A beautiful, but devious smile crossed Maxine's red lips. "Ah, they are the special ones. The ones born with an uncanny ability to produce the enzyme at an amazing rate. They are a perpetual source of what keeps me alive. And, so, I keep them in this insensate state of existence as a backup... always the same, never aging, always the children they were when they first encountered me."

"How old are you, monster?" Sophie wanted to know. "A hundred years old? Two?"

Maxine was amused by her questions. "Dear lady, I have lived through times you have only read of in your planet's history books. The building of the pyramids, the Crusades, the Industrial Age, terrorism, war upon war upon war. Since the era I was stranded here, I have feasted with pharaohs and kings, lived among the rich and famous. That is why I cannot be defeated. My knowledge is so much more advanced than yours. I am like an elephant existing among the lowly ant."

Phillip Mitchell directed the muzzle of his Remington toward the woman. "Let's see how the elephant holds up to a blast of double-aught buckshot between its eyes."

"Have you abandoned your Hippocratic Oath, Doctor?" Maxine's eyes sparkled. "It doesn't matter, though. You will never be able to pull the trigger." The thing sighed deeply and a faint shimmer seemed to surround the being's feminine form... a release of vapor that was nearly undetectable... at least by the human eye.

Abruptly, an odor began to drift throughout the factory, subdued at first, then growing in intensity. A bitter, skunky stench like marigolds. "The masks!" called Kyle. As he raised the mask to his face, the fingers of his hands had already began to tingle and grow numb.

The thing laughed loudly... its human voice changing into the moist, bubbly resonance of its true self. "Those coverings won't protect you. True, my venom works more effectively through the respiratory system... but, eventually, it will enter the pores of your skin. And we will end this annoying little intrusion that you've brought about."

The three began to feel the effects of the poison as it attacked their nerves and the functions of their internal organs. The strength began to drain from their muscles and their thoughts grew sluggish and disjointed.

They watched in horror as Miss Maxine began to expand. The smooth, unblemished skin of delicate latex split, showing glistening gray flesh underneath. The human garment began to shred and fall away, as the true form of the creature took shape. Soon, tatters of rubber flesh and clothing lay across the oil-stained concrete of the mill floor. The thing—large, gray, and bloated—rose to a height of eight feet and towered over them. Its thick, ropey veins throbbed and pulsated as fluid the hue and consistency of filthy motor oil coursed through its arteries. Its yellow, purple-veined eyes bulged, as its sharp, black teeth snapped and grated one against the other.

Kyle tried to raise the Mossberg, but the shotgun seemed too heavy in his hands. He looked over at Phillip. The doctor was having the same problem. Their sinew and muscle was incapacitated and refused to work properly. *Oh, God,* he thought, as his vision began to blur. *Don't let it do this to us... please.*

Then he raised his head and saw Sophie Taylor standing there, facing the massive, gray creature, no more than seven feet between them. He watched, confused, as she reached inside the big bag that hung from her left shoulder. Her dark hand emerged holding a large plastic bag. A bag filled with a grainy, white substance.

Is she crazy? What the hell is she doing?

As the monster loomed over her, preparing to descend and attack, Sophie opened the bag and slung its contents directly at the glistening, gray body of the creature. Something akin to a shrill, high-pitched shriek filled the building, rising to the rafters and rattling the metal sheets of the factory walls. The white powder clung to the gray flesh of the thing but didn't remain where it was. Instead, it seemed to sink into the skin of the thing that had once been Mister Mack. The substance was dissolving its flesh like acid, revealing the stringy white muscles that lay underneath. Slowly, the creature's bulk began to decrease and a nasty, black fluid—its life blood—began to seep, then spurt, from the open wounds that covered its alien body.

As the creature perished, the odor of marigolds began to decrease. Strength and control replaced the weakness and insensitivity the men had felt moments before. As Sophie retrieved a second bag of powder from her bag and lobbed it toward the creature's wailing head, Kyle and Phillip Mitchell rushed in and began to pump round after round of buckshot into the body of the otherworldly parasite. As its outer layer disintegrated and liquefied, projectiles from the shotguns ripped and rented the sinew, muscle, and bones that were exposed.

By the time the plastic bags and the two 12-gauge shotguns were empty, the thing they knew as Mister Mack was dead. It lay in a great, gelatinous heap that settled and spread across the cement floor of the mill. The three of them stood there, shaken and exhausted, amazed that it was finally over.

"Sophie," asked Kyle. "What was in the bag?"

The elderly woman smiled. "Salt. Nothing but plain, ordinary table salt."

"What?" The two men stared at her in disbelief.

"When I was a young'un, there was a swamp near our home," she told them. "We children would wade and play in it, as children tend to do without thinking, and we'd come home with leeches stuck all up and down our legs. Our mama would take the Morton salt down out of the kitchen cabinet and sprinkle it all over those nasty bloodsuckers. That salt would start dissolving their skin and they'd drop right off. When Mack took me as a child, I saw it for what it was... a type of parasite similar to the ones that dwelled in the swamp. I reached out and touched its skin right before I passed out. It was like touching the moist black flesh of a swamp leech."

"Well, I'll be damned," said Kyle. He stared at the remains of Mister Mack for a long moment, then turned back to the children suspended in blue light.

"Let's see what we can do," said Phillip.

Soon, they figured how to deactivate the suspension beam. Instead of turning off the generator and having them all drop to the floor and risk injury, Mitchell interrupted the bottom of the beam of each pod with a sheet of plywood, while Kyle caught the released child in mid-air and lowered them gently to the ground. The first one they rescued was Hannah Spaulding.

"Mr. Sadler," she murmured, weak and disoriented. "Where did you come from?"

"I came looking for you," he told her.

"Where... where is Becky?"

"Don't you worry. She's just fine."

She nodded sluggishly. "Good." Then she fell into a peaceful slumber.

One after the other, they liberated twelve more. When they reached the fourteenth, Kyle stopped in his tracks.

"What is it?" asked Sophie.

"It's... it's Jimmy."

They deactivated the beam and, gently, Kyle took the twelve-year-old boy in his arms. As he lowered him to the floor, tears came swiftly and he began to weep.

"Who are you?" Jimmy Johnson asked softly.

"I'm a friend of Kyle," he told him. "He sent me to fetch you."

"Why are you crying, mister?"

"Just glad to see you, I guess."

Confused, the boy frowned. "Well, quit it, will you? Don't be such a wimp, okay?"

Kyle couldn't help but laugh. "Anything you say, buddy."

Sophie knelt beside the boy and watched over him as Kyle and Phillip moved on to the others.

Kyle stood in front of the Johnsons' front door for a long moment before he finally knocked.

Soon, a middle-aged woman opened the door and smiled warmly at him. "Kyle. How are you?"

"I'm fine, Mrs. Johnson," he replied, returning the smile. He remembered how she had been when he was a kid... young, beautiful, and movie-star blond... practically his second mom from age six to twelve. It had all changed after her son's disappearance. Fear, grief, and uncertainty had taken its toll on her and she had aged rapidly. She was fifty-five now instead of thirty, but looked more like she was in her late sixties. Kyle remembered seeing her around town during his teenage and young adult years– gray and unsmiling, the life nearly sucked clean out of her. Her smile had returned, as well as that happy, carefree expression he remembered from a quarter century ago, but, unfortunately, her youth was lost forever. "Is Jimmy ready?"

"Almost. He'll be out in a minute." She stared at him for a long moment. Tears bloomed in her eyes and she reached out to embrace him. As they held each other, she whispered in his ear. "Thank you, Kyle. Thank you bringing him back to us."

Kyle swallowed dryly and simply nodded. It was difficult to talk, to even think about what Jimmy's return meant to them... as well as him.

Mrs. Johnson pulled away, wiped her eyes, and smiled once again. Then stepped back inside.

Kyle turned and stood on the Johnsons' front porch, nervous, his hands crammed in his jacket pockets. He hadn't been this keyed up when he had proposed to Gloria.

"Hey."

He turned to see Jimmy standing in the doorway, dressed in a Captain America costume. He had a plastic jack-o'-lantern pail in his right hand. Kyle recognized it from the last time the two of them had gone trick-or-treating... an eternity ago.

"Hey, buddy," he said. "Going as Cap, I see. No Freddy or Jason this year?"

Jimmy Johnson lowered his eyes to the floorboards of the porch. "No. I reckon I've had my fill of monsters for a while."

"Yes. I can certainly understand that. So... how are you doing?"

Jimmy shrugged. "Okay, I guess. It's been... you know... *weird*."

Kyle felt himself choking up, but fought to keep his composure. "Do you want to sit down for a minute... shoot the shit square between the eyes?" It was an expression that he and Jimmy had once shared.

The twelve-year-old nodded. "Okay." He sat on the front porch steps and Kyle sat down next to him.

They said nothing for nearly a minute. Then Jimmy stared him square in the face. "It's hard to believe that it's really you. I mean, you sort of look like Kyle, but older. A lot older."

"I know it's strange... and difficult. It's hard for me, too." Kyle considered something he had been turning over in his mind for several days now. "Let me tell you a couple of things and maybe it'll help you... to believe that I'm really who I am."

"Okay." Jimmy flashed that crooked grin that Kyle remembered so well. "Go on and shoot the shit."

"Well... remember when we were ten? You sneaked a couple of old *Penthouse* magazines out of your uncle's Army footlocker? We spent most of that afternoon in that clubhouse we built down by Cedar Creek, looking at all those naked women... and vowed we'd never have anything to do with girls because they looked so gross without their clothes."

Jimmy's ears grew red and he giggled. "Yeah... I remember."

"And that time we decided we were going to pull a heist at

Mr. Carver's drugstore? We snuck a couple of candy bars from the display right in front of his register and got them into our pockets before he could see us. I got a Baby Ruth and you got a Kit Kat. We left the drugstore and got halfway home before we felt guilty as hell and went straight back. Put that candy back right where we got it. Years later, Mr. Carver told me that he knew that we'd lifted them, but didn't say anything. He knew we were good boys... that we'd do the right thing, after we gave it some thought."

Jimmy looked over at him and smiled. "It really is you."

"Yeah. Still goofy, old Kyle. Still your best friend."

"Really?" the boy asked, his eyes hopeful.

"That never changed, Jimmy... even after you were gone. It never will."

A frightened expression crossed the boy's freckled face. "Kyle... what am I going to do? How am I going to deal with this? Mom and Dad... they're more like my grandparents now. And the world... it's so different. Look at all the *Star Wars* movies they've made since I've been gone. And the math at school... it's totally screwed up now!"

"It's going to be weird, trying to sort things out," Kyle explained. "I have some things to work out, too... things I need to accept... as well as let go of. We can do it together, if you want. I'm here for you... if you'll do the same for me."

"Okay, Mister... uh, Kyle." Jimmy blushed and grinned. "Sorry about that."

"That's all right." He looked toward the street. The sun was setting and there were already trick-or-treaters gathering to make their nocturnal rounds. He thought of Becky, still in the hospital, but doing much better. Doctor Mitchell had even said she would probably be able to go home in a day or two. "My daughter isn't going to be able to do Halloween this year, so I thought, what the heck... maybe I'd spend it with another really cool kid."

"Then let's get our butts in gear and get some candy!" laughed Jimmy. He picked up the pumpkin pail and bounded down the steps to the sidewalk.

Kyle smiled and, not quite as swiftly, rose from his place on the steps and joined him. "You've got a deal, pal. But, remember, I get dibs on the Baby Ruths."

They would have liked to have said that nothing had changed at all... that it was just like old times again. But neither dared to utter that sentiment, perhaps afraid of losing what they mutually shared that night. Soon, those twenty-five lost years between them melted and faded away, until absolutely nothing awkward or unusual remained.

Together, they headed into the cool October night, laughing and cutting up and shooting the shit right between the eyes.

BLOOD SUEDE SHOES

Ruby Paquette was walking home from the big Halloween rock and roll show in Baton Rouge, when the headlights of a car cut through the moonless night. They blazed like the luminous eyes of a demon cat, casting a pale glow upon the two-lane highway and the swampy thicket to either side. She turned and regarded the approaching vehicle, squinting against the glare. The car sounded like a predator. Its big eight-cylinder engine seemed to rumble and roar with an appetite for something more than oil and gasoline.

The crimson '58 Cadillac began to slow when the headlights revealed her short, dumpy form walking along the gravel shoulder. She was dressed like a bobby soxer, her dark hair tied into a ponytail, a monogrammed white blouse, poodle skirt, and two-tone saddle shoes... the whole works. Everything that, in reality, she was not.

Ruby turned her back to the headlights and kept going. She stared straight ahead, following her own expanding shadow and the whitewashed borderline beside the highway. As the automobile slowed to a creep and prepared to pull alongside her, Ruby chanced a quick glance over her shoulder. The illusion of a ravenous feline was compounded by the Caddy's front grillwork. It leered at her with a mouthful of polished chrome fangs.

"Hey, sugar!" called a man's voice from the convertible. "Can I give you a ride somewhere? Kinda late for a beauty like you to be out all by your lonesome."

Beauty? Ruby bristled at the word, especially when it was directed at her. She was no beauty and she knew it. She was just a homely Cajun girl; an overweight, acne-ravaged teenager with limp black hair and jelly-jar eyeglasses. How could the driver of the expensive car have made such a stupid mistake? True, he probably hadn't seen her face yet, but he didn't really need to. One glimpse of her squat, elephantine body waddling down the road should have told him that she was certainly no beauty.

"No, thanks," she called back to him. "I don't have far to go." She was aware that the Caddy was almost at a standstill now, inching its way beside her. She twisted her face toward the tangle of swamp beyond the road. *Please, God, just let him drive on by,* she thought to herself. *I don't want him to see how much of a dog I really am.*

"Aw, come on, darlin'," urged the driver. He was right alongside her now. "Let ol' Reb give you a ride home."

It was the dawning familiarity of the voice, as well as the mention of his name, that made Ruby's stomach clench with excitement. She looked around and, yes, it *was* him. It was Rockabilly Reb in the flesh!

"You know who I am, don't you, sugar?" grinned Reb, flashing that pearly smile that was becoming increasingly famous in the South and beyond.

"Yeah," said Ruby in bewilderment. "You're Rockabilly Reb. I saw you at the Louisiana Hayride tonight."

"And I saw you, too."

Reb winked at her—actually winked at *her*—Rumpy Ruby, as her peers in high school were cruelly fond of calling her.

"Third row, fifth girl to the left... right?" Reb asked. "Sitting between the Wicked Witch and the ballerina."

"Right." Ruby blushed, feeling the heat of embarrassment blossom in her full cheeks. She stopped walking and stood, wondering if her encounter was actually a dream. She crossed her thick arms and pinched herself through her sweater. No, it was really happening. She was actually talking, face-to-face, with a genuine rockabilly singer.

"Well, how about it, sugar? Gonna let me play the Good Samaritan this fine Halloween night and give you a lift home? I was heading in that direction anyway." Reb's immaculate smile hadn't faltered in the least. It seemed to be a part of his natural charm.

Ruby looked ahead toward the three miles of swamp that stretched between Baton Rouge and her bayou home, then back to the idling Cadillac and the offer of getting there in style and comfort. What was she going to say, "No, thanks, but I'd rather walk"? This was the bad boy of rock and roll—the potential heir to the heartthrob throne left empty after Elvis Presley had been unexpectedly drafted into the Army earlier that year. Her mother was forever drumming the rule of never riding with strangers into her mind, but to pass up such a golden opportunity would be pure madness. It wasn't every day that a chubby wallflower got the chance to cruise with a certified superstar.

"Okay," she said. Ruby opened the passenger door of the car and climbed inside. The seats were of smooth, crimson leather, as was the rest of the interior. From the rearview mirror dangled a set of fuzzy dice, jet black with bright red spots like tiny eyes peeking through the dark fur. She settled onto the seat next to the driver, feeling the coolness of the upholstery against the back of her thighs. That, along with the thrumming vibration of the Caddy's big engine, sparked a naughty sensation deep down inside her. It was the same sensation of arousal that she got at night, when she lay awake in her bed and thought about Will Knox, the high school quarterback, and the time she had passed the boys' locker room and caught a fleeting glimpse of him, completely naked, just before the door shut.

"Ready to go?" asked Rockabilly Reb.

"Sure," said Ruby. "There's a turnoff about a mile down the road. I live a couple of miles back in the swamp there."

Reb nodded and sent the big convertible roaring down the highway. The singer flashed a glance at his young passenger. "So, you're a bobby soxer, are you?"

Ruby's face turned beet read. She looked down at her clothing. She knew the outfit looked silly, especially on a fat cow like her. "No," she blurted self-consciously, "I just dressed like this because, well, you know, it's Halloween."

Reb flashed another smile that turned her heart to jelly. "No, you're not the bobby soxer type. I'd say you're a genuine rock and roll beauty. No doubt about it."

Again, that twinge of bitter anger. "Why do you keep calling me that? I'm not pretty at all. Are you making fun of me or something?"

The singer shook his head. "Why, I'd never do a thing like that, darlin'. I wouldn't hurt one of my fans for anything in the world. True, you may not be a Marilyn Monroe or Jayne Mansfield, but you do have your own inner beauty. You know how a candy bar looks like a dog turd when you tear off the wrapper? It doesn't look very appetizing at all, does it? But when you bite into it, it's just as delicious as can be. That's how some girls are. They ain't so pretty on the outside, but underneath they're honest-to-goodness beauties."

Reb's simple explanation put Ruby at ease. She pushed her shyness aside for a moment and studied the man sitting next to her. He looked a little different than he did up on that stage surrounded by klieg lights and a blaring sound system. Up there he looked like a wild Adonis, clad in sparkling red, white, and blue. But here in the car, Reb seemed less glamorous and more than a little exhausted. His bleached-blond hair looked frizzled and lank, like corn silk that had withered beneath a hot August sun. His lean face seemed pale and lined with the weariness of long, sleepless miles on the road. Even his trademark costume had seen better days. Up close, the rhinestone coat with a rebel flag emblazoned on the back seemed dull and lackluster. And his red suede shoes—the opposite of Carl Perkins's famed blue ones—looked scuffed and rusty, like blood that had congealed and dried to an ugly brown crust.

Thunder rumbled in the dense clouds overhead and a few drops of rain began to hit them. "Looks like we're in for a real downpour," Reb said. He pushed a button on the Caddy's dash and the top began to unfold behind the back seat and rise slowly over them. By the time Reb fastened the clips to the top of the windshield, the bottom fell out. Great sheets of water crashed earthward, drenching southern Louisiana with their wet fury.

Reb turned off where Ruby told him to, but they had gone only a quarter of a mile into the black tangle of the swamp when the rain cut their visibility down to nothing. "I reckon we'd better park for a while and wait out the storm. Wouldn't want to make a wrong turn and end up in the swamp as some hungry gator's trick-or-treat snack."

"I reckon not." Ruby sat there, her bashfulness pushing her to the limits of the seat and pressing her against the passenger door.

"How about a little music to pass the time?" Reb turned on the AM radio. Chuck Berry's "Johnny B. Goode" was winding down and next up was Rockabilly Reb's newest single, "Rock and Roll Anatomy Lesson."

"A little bit of heart, a little bit of soul,
A little bit of mind, and a whole lotta rock and roll..."

"What a coincidence!" Reb laughed.

Ruby sat listening to the monotonous drumming of rain on the roof and the haunting melody of Reb's electric guitar. After the song ended and the Everly Brothers' "Bird Dog" began, Ruby eyed the grinning rocker with wonderment. "I can't believe that I'm really here... sitting right next to you."

"Well, you are, Ruby." Reb's smile glowed dashboard green in the darkness.

The girl returned his smile, then frowned just as quickly. "How did you know my name was Ruby? I didn't tell you it was."

Reb shrugged. "I don't know. You just look like a Ruby, that's all."

Smoothly, he changed the subject. "So, how did you like the show tonight?"

"It was great!" Ruby thought back to the three-hour Louisiana Hayride that had featured big names like gravel-voiced Johnny Cash, piano-playing Fats Domino, and, of course, Rockabilly Reb. "You were the best, though." She smiled demurely. "I think you're even better than Elvis."

Reb chuckled. "Well, that's mighty high praise, darlin'. But I reckon I must have disappointed some folks on those last couple of songs I did. My voice was kinda going out on me and my guitar-picking was a bit off."

Ruby recalled the last two numbers: "High School Honey"

and "Bayou Boogie". Reb's voice had been unusually flat and his normally hot guitar licks seemed strangely off-key. She had attributed it to the rigors of being on the road too long, driving from gig to gig without time to rest.

"Want me to sing you a song, Ruby?"

The bespectacled girl felt her heart leap with joy. "Sure!" Again, she couldn't quite believe that she was here, stranded in a violent downpour with her idol. And now he was going to sing to her!

Rockabilly Reb reached into the back seat and found his guitar. It was a sunburst Les Paul Special—a custom-made model for the left-handed player. He slipped the sparkling rhinestone strap around his neck. The sickly green glow of the dashboard light played upon the taut strings of the instrument and the glittering spangles of his gaudy jacket, illuminating the interior of the car with an eerie light.

"Sorry I can't hook up my amplifier, but we'll just have to make do the best we can. So, what would you like to hear? What's your favorite Rockabilly Reb song?"

Ruby smiled. "Forever Baby," she said without hesitation.

Reb grinned. "That's my favorite, too. Here goes..." He began to strum on the unplugged guitar, producing a series of metallic cords that could scarcely be heard above the rainstorm.

"Ruby, Ruby, be my forever baby...
Ruby, Ruby, be my forever lady...
Ruby, baby, tell me you'll be mine."

The teenager was a little startled. He was using her own name in place of the customary one. Sitting there listening to him, Ruby couldn't quite remember whose name originally had embellished the lyrics. Sometimes it sounded like Lucy, sometimes like Judy or Trudy. Every time she heard the song on the radio or on the jukebox in the soda shop in town, it seemed as though Reb sang about a different girl. But that was impossible. The record company wouldn't allow him to cut alternate versions of the same hit, using a different name each time.

After he was finished, he sat back and grinned that

country-boy grin of his. "I know, I was a little off-key, but it's been a long night and I'm kinda tired."

"It was perfect," Ruby said. "You know, I always wondered how you got your start. I hadn't even heard of you until the first of the year, and now here you are a big star and all."

"It wasn't an easy row to hoe, I'll tell you that." Reb lost his smile for the first time since he'd picked her up. "Started out as a guy who was long on good looks, but mighty short on talent."

"I can't believe that," she said.

"Well, it's the God's honest truth, sugar-pie. I saw all those fellas out there making records and money by the fistfuls, and I figured to get in on the action. And I thought I had a good chance, too, but there were others who thought otherwise. I went up there to Sun Records once, and you know what old Sam Phillips told me? He said, 'You got the look, boy, and you got the moves, but you ain't got a lick of natural-born talent. You can't pick a guitar, can't tickle the ivories, and can't sing a note without sounding like a year-old calf with its privates hung up in a barbwire fence.' I must admit, it was pretty darned discouraging, that trip to Memphis."

"But he was wrong, wasn't he?"

"No, Ruby, dear, that man was right on the mark. I had no talent at all, except for looking pretty and grinning like a happy jackass. I figured I'd have to just face the fact that I wasn't gonna make it in the music business. Then, when I was drowning my sorrows in a honky-tonk on Union Street, I made the acquaintance of my present manager, Colonel Darker."

"You mean Colonel *Parker*, don't you? Elvis's manager?"

"No, Darker is the complete opposite. He's an oily little rat of a fella, but he has a good head for business. He sat down at the bar and asked me what was wrong. I told him, and he made me the strangest offer I ever heard. Said he'd make me a bona fide rock and roll star if I'd sign my soul over to him. I thought it was pretty darned funny at the time. I mean, I'd heard of such corny lines before, but only on spooky radio shows and in those EC comics before they were banned. Well, since I was half drunk and didn't figure I'd need that no-account soul of mine anyway, I agreed. I signed the contract on the spot, and then he took me

out to the parking lot. He gave me the keys to this apple-red
Cadillac, as well as the costume you see me wearing and the
guitar I'm holding here. He also told me what I'd have to do to
get the talent to be a star. At first, I didn't want to have no part of
it, but soon my hunger for money and fame got the best of me."

Ruby felt her skin crawl with a sudden shiver. "What... what
did you have to do?" Something deep down inside her wanted
to know, while another part didn't.

Rockabilly Reb smiled, and this time it possessed a disturbing quality—a quality that had been there all along, only
hidden. "Tell me something, Ruby," he said in a voice that was
barely a whisper. "Do you believe what all those hellfire preach-
ers say about rock and roll? Do you believe that it's unwhole-
some and unclean? That it's the Devil's music?"

"No, of course not," stammered Ruby. "That's just silly talk
by a bunch of holy rollers. Rock and roll is just plain fun, that's
all."

"I'm afraid you're wrong about that, dumpling. Rock and
roll *can* be safe and fun, but it can also be dark and perilous.
The grown-ups, they can sense something is basically dangerous about the music, but they can't quite put their finger on it.
Most of the time the music is sung by decent, God-fearing boys
like Elvis and Roy Orbison and Carl Perkins, to name a few. I
don't know about Jerry Lee. That old boy has a mean streak a
country mile long."

Ruby said nothing. She just pressed her back against the
passenger door and listened to him ramble on. Inconspicuously,
her chubby hand fumbled for the door handle, but, strangely
enough, she couldn't find it. The inner panel of the door was
smooth... and warm to the touch.

"I'm one of the first of the truly dangerous ones," he told
her. His pale blue eyes blazed with the madness of desperation. "My talent wasn't a gift from God, but from Satan himself.
Colonel Darker likes rock and roll because it reminds him of
Hell. All those girls screaming and hollering, well, that's just
how the Bible describes purgatory—weeping and wailing and
gnashing of teeth.

"The Colonel, he's given me fortune and fame... as well as

power. And when someone gets in the way of my success, I get riled up. I went up north recently and auditioned for a winter tour that's coming up with Buddy Holly, Ritchie Valens, and the Big Bopper. But they turned me down. Said I was too much of a vulgar hillbilly to appeal to Midwestern teenagers. Well, they'll learn their mistake soon enough. Me and the Colonel are gonna cook up a little surprise. Those boys are gonna climb to the top, only to fall... and fall mighty damned hard, too."

Ruby believed every word he said. She watched in growing horror as Reb's eyes lost their natural blueness and took on a muted crimson hue, like a smoldering coal wavering between living fire and dying ash. Behind her back, her hand continued to search for the door handle, but still she was unsuccessful in finding it.

"You know where I get my talent?" asked the rocker. "The human soul. But not from my own... no, the Colonel has my own damned soul under lock and key. That was stipulated in the contract. Instead, I must have the soul of an innocent, the truly beautiful essence of an unsoiled virgin to give me the power I need to rock and roll."

It was at that moment that Ruby noticed that the head of the electric guitar was not like that of other instruments. It was wickedly pointed at the end and honed to razor sharpness. Reb gripped the neck of the guitar and began to lower it, directing it toward the center of her broad chest. She screamed and tried to push up on the rag-top roof of the Caddy. Her hands recoiled in repulsion. The underside of the roof was sticky with warm, wet slime.

"Let me sing you a song," Rockabilly Reb rasped.

Then the blade of the guitar was inside her, slicing through her blouse and the elastic of her bra, then past soft flesh and the hardness of her breastbone. As her heart exploded, Ruby heard the song Rockabilly Reb had sung to her only moments before. But this time it came with a savage ferocity that originated from a realm commanded by the notorious Colonel Darker.

"RUBY, RUBY, BE MY FOREVER BABY... RUBY, RUBY, BE MY FOREVER LADY... RUBY, BABY, TELL ME YOU'LL BE MINE!"

"No!" she screamed. She watched in mounting panic as her life's blood flooded the floorboards of the car in great, sluggish pools. It was instantly absorbed by Reb's red suede shoes, which pulsed with a life of their own, bulging with dark veins as they drank in the crimson fluid. Reb's costume took on a new brilliance, sparkling with an unholy inner fire. His face lost its pallor. His skin grew tanned and robust. The head of lifeless hair grew fuller and lighter in hue, until it blazed like white-hot steel.

"TELL ME!" shrieked the singer. "TELL ME, RUBY! TELL ME YOU'LL BE MINE!"

Ruby could feel the guitar strings strumming within her body, sending sonic notes of utter agony throughout her tubby frame. She opened her mouth to scream in protest, but she no longer possessed a tongue to vent her awful terror. The vibrations from the hellish instrument racked her spine and blossomed with deadly force into the chamber of her skull. There was a moment of incredible pressure and then her ears and mouth gave explosive birth to her brain. She felt her eyes shoot from their sockets with such force that the lenses of her glasses shattered.

Rockabilly Reb's demonic song grew in intensity and her empty skull became the guitar's makeshift amplifier. Waves of trebled sound flowed from the orifices of her head, turning the inside of the Cadillac into a concert hall for the damned. Then, as the ballad came to an end, she felt her soul being siphoned from her body, channeled through the strings, into the wooden body of the Les Paul.

As unconsciousness took her into its dark and comforting folds, Ruby knew that there was no longer any use in struggling. She mouthed a single word in answer to Reb's evil chorus… a silent *yes*. And, although she could neither see nor hear, she knew that the rocker's voice was rising in a howl of triumph and his grin stretched wide with a renewed power born of a spirit that was not his own.

Colonel Darker was right. It *was* like Hell.

The screams, the writhing bodies, the pressing heat of the

spotlights and the crowd: it filled the high school auditorium like a crazed purgatory confined within four walls. She and Rockabilly Reb were at center stage, engulfed in the dancing flames of youthful passion.

She sensed the Colonel standing in the wings, watching the show. She loathed the man as much as she loathed her treacherous lover. She could sense his eyes upon the crowd, enjoying the thrashing of young bodies and the shrill shrieks of females torn between teenage infatuation and womanly lust. She had been among them once, but that seemed like an eternity ago. She had not been beautiful like most of these squealing girls. She had been burdened with an ugly and cumbersome body, but at least it had been one of flesh and bone, and not one constructed of gleaming steel and polished wood, like the one she now possessed.

Rockabilly Reb finished the song and stood before the microphone, letting the screams of wild adoration engulf him. He glanced at his manager and gave the man a wink. Colonel Darker nodded and, with a wolfish grin, merged with the backstage shadows.

"Thank you very much," said Reb, sending the crowed into a renewed frenzy with a flash of his smile. "Here's one of my biggest hits and one of your favorites."

He began to sing...

"Ruby, Ruby, be my forever baby...
Ruby, Ruby, be my forever lady...
Ruby, baby, tell me you'll be mine."

It was her song and she had grown to despise it. During the past few weeks, it had thrummed through her new body, bringing pangs of disgust and despair rather than the rapture of undying passion. The promise of eternal love was a lie. Others had shared the song before her and there would be others afterward. It was only hers until the essence of her captured soul faded like a faltering flame.

As Rockabilly Reb's nimble fingers caressed her taut strings, bringing forth the hot licks of demon rock and roll, she could restrain herself no longer. She screamed out in tortured anguish, hoping that at least one of the teenyboppers in the crowd would hear the cry and recognize it as a warning.

But her torment fell on deaf ears. It emerged as the piercing squeal of feedback, then was swallowed up by the blare of the music.

And the damned rocked on.

CLOWN TREATS

They were halfway into their trick-or-treating, when they reached McLaren Avenue.

"Hey, let's go to Mrs. Abernathy's house first," suggested Andy.

The other two—Madison and Jeff—agreed enthusiastically. Their fifth-grade teacher, Helen Abernathy, always had the best treats on the block. Not crappy stuff like bubble gum or Dum Dum suckers, but the good stuff like fun-size Snickers and Baby Ruths, and sometimes cool candy like Pop Rocks or Fun Dip. And she wasn't stingy, either. She usually deposited a heaping handful into their bags, especially if you were one of her students.

They marched down the sidewalk to the two-story white house in the center of McLaren. Andy was dressed as Captain Jack Sparrow, Madison as Wonder Woman, and Jeff as Negan from *The Walking Dead*. Their bags—the big, sturdy Brach's Candy sacks that Mr. Wilkes gave out at the drugstore every Halloween—were only an eighth of the way full. They knew Mrs. Abernathy's generosity would boost that amount significantly, by a quarter pound at least.

They reached the house and opened the gate of the white picket fence. The front porch light glowed invitingly, beckoning them. They walked up the concrete walkway, mounted the porch steps, and approached the door.

Jeff reached out and rang the doorbell with Lucille—a plastic Wiffle Ball bat spray-painted blood red and wrapped with silver floral wire from his mom's flower shop. "Trick or treat!" they called out, laughing.

When no one came to the door, Andy reached out and

knocked. The moment his knuckles touched the wooden panel, the door swung slowly inward.

They looked at one another. Madison shrugged and tentatively pushed it open. "Mrs. Abernathy?"

Beyond the doorway stretched the Abernathy living room. It was dark, except for a single lamp at the far corner of the room. As they stepped inside, they were startled to see a shadowy form sitting in a large, leather recliner. Even in the gloom they could make out the figure's features.

It was a clown. A rather large and rotund one. His costume was bright yellow, red, and blue, and his shoes were a good eighteen inches with the toes slightly curled at the ends. His face was ghostly white with blue and green highlights and his foam nose was round and red. Completing the ensemble was a rainbow-colored afro wig.

"Happy Halloween, kids!" he greeted. A white-gloved hand motioned for them to approach. "Come on in. We've been expecting you."

Madison pressed her hand against her chest and giggled. "Mr. Abernathy! You scared us half to death!"

The clown pouted and wagged a finger at her. "It's Chuckles to you, young lady."

"Okay... Chuckles." The girl's eyes struggled to see in the gloom. "Where's Mrs. Abernathy?"

Chuckles grinned broadly. His eyes glinted like bits of sharp metal in the dim glow of the living room lamp. "Oh... she's around somewhere." He regarded the three children. "Come closer... let me take a look at you."

Although they felt a little weird having already entered the Abernathy house, they did as they were told. The clown leaned forward and appraised the fifth graders. "So, you're Helen's students?" he asked.

"Yes, sir," said Andy. "Mrs. Abernathy is our favorite teacher."

Chuckles laughed. It was a strange sound, bearing more sarcasm than humor. "Why, of course she is! After all, you are her *class*! Her precious children... the love her life... the reason she does what she does, day after day." The three couldn't be sure, but it seemed like there was a strong tone of resentment in the man's voice.

Madison took a step backward when the man belched loudly. She could tell that he had been drinking. Not beer. No, this was something much stronger. Sort of like the bottle of Jack Daniel's her father and her uncle broke out after Thanksgiving dinner every November. The stench of alcohol seemed to literally reek from the man's pores.

"I guess you're ready for some treats, aren't you?" He leered through his mask of pale greasepaint. "Well, come closer."

They took a couple of steps.

He grinned in the gloom. "Closer."

Andy looked at Madison and she at Jeff. It was clear that the same thing was on each of their minds: *We should really get out of here.*

On the floor, between the clown's oversized feet, was a large black trash bag—the big fifty-gallon lawn type you buy at Home Depot. His gloved hands dipped into the bag and disappeared from sight. "You know, you children—her wonderful *students*—are all she ever talks about. How smart you are, how witty and sharp. Never mind that I want to talk about work or football or any of *my* interests. It's always about *you*. She never thinks about my wants or needs. Just her twenty-three little elementary school angels."

Jeff looked toward the staircase and the upstairs landing above. Both were dark and motionless. *Where is she?* he thought. *Are she and Mr. Abernathy playing a joke on us?*

"I... I think we ought to be going," Madison said, echoing the other two's thoughts.

Chuckles acted like he hadn't heard her. "She stays up well past bedtime every night, grading homework and making lesson plans. And where am I? Alone in bed, waiting for her. Most nights I can't even stay awake to kiss her goodnight. But do you think that bothers her? Hell, no. After all, it's all about her precious class. That's what matters most."

Uncomfortably, the three backed up a couple of steps.

The clown's eyes widened a little, looking glazed and

disoriented. *I think he's going to pass out or something*, Andy thought to himself.

But he didn't. "You know what she says? She always says 'It's my duty to encourage and inspire them. Sure, they're only in the fifth grade, but they are so bright and inquisitive, they could grow up to be anything. A doctor, a scientist... even the president of the United States. I want to make an impression that will set their futures in motion... give them a little bit of me to carry around for the rest of their lives'. I always thought that was bullshit. But you know what? I agree with her now. I think that's exactly what she oughta do."

They backed up a few steps more. Madison glanced over her shoulder. The front door—still standing open—seemed a mile away.

Chuckle's tiny eyes seemed to refocus. "Where do you think you're going? Come here."

"Mister Abernathy... we've really gotta..."

"I said... *come here.*"

Frightened, they did as he said.

"Now hold out your bags," he instructed. "Mrs. Abernathy told me to give you something special... along with a message from her."

"Uh...okay," stammered Jeff. He held his candy sack open. The paper of the sack rattled in his trembling hands.

Chuckles the Clown grinned broadly, showing off nasty, tobacco-stained teeth. He dipped into the trash bag and brought something out, dropping it into the depths of Jeff's bag. It was so dark in the living room that the boy couldn't tell exactly what it was. A plastic bag of some kind.

"Mrs. Abernathy says that twelve inches equals one foot."

As Jeff stepped away, Madison approached him. The treat was deposited into her sack, heavy enough to cause her bag to sag. "Mrs. Abernathy says that you deserve a big hand, for helping sharpen her pencils and keeping her blackboard erased and clean."

Then it was Andy's turn. It took two hands to dig his treat from the depths of the lawn bag. When it was dropped into his sack, it felt as if a bowling ball had been placed there. "Mrs.

Abernathy wants you to excel in your studies. To study your lessons and always get ahead."

The three kids stood there for a moment, unsure of what to do next.

Chuckles laughed loudly. It had a ring to it that was utterly devoid of humor or good will. "Well, what are you waiting for? You got what you came for. Now get the hell out of here."

Without further hesitation, they did as they were told. A moment later they were away from that shadowy living room and outside again. They leapt down the steps and made it to the sidewalk below. Inside the house, they could hear Mr. Abernathy, aka Chuckles, laughing and talking to himself.

They reached the leaf-strewn avenue of McLaren and stood there in the pale glow of the streetlights.

Jeff laughed nervously. "That was so *weird!*"

"I'll say!" said Andy. "What did he give us anyway? Mine feels like it weighs a ton!"

"I don't know." Madison reached into her bag and felt around. She found the corner of the plastic bag and lifted it. It was heavy... sloshing with sluggish liquid.

She nearly had it out of her treat bag when the streetlight overhead shone on its contents. The halogen glow revealed pale, white flesh and the sparkling gleam of a diamond wedding ring. The fingernails were painted Malibu Blush Pink... Mrs. Abernathy's favorite color.

Andy watched as the girl dropped the plastic bag and flung the sack to the ground. Her face was bleached with shock. He turned and saw a dark stain blossom across the front of Jeff's blue jeans as his friend stared into his own treat bag and moaned.

Almost afraid to look, Andy glanced down into his trick-or-treat sack. His plastic bag was larger than theirs, the big two-gallon size. The zip-lock edges had come loose, and a strand of curly copper hair protruded from the gap. He was familiar with that particular hue, for he saw it every day, Monday through Friday, from eight o'clock am to two-forty-five pm.

Horrified, the three abandoned their bags and ran home as fast as their feet could carry them.

The police arrived at the Abernathy home twenty minutes

later, but Chuckles the Clown was nowhere to be found.

They would search for him for most of that Halloween night before they finally found him.

After all, he had a school classroom roster and many more treats to deliver.

THE CISTERN

Surprisingly, it was the same as he last remembered.

Well, *almost* the same. Of course, there would have to be changes after twenty years. The old Ridgeland Theatre had been replaced with a new grocery store and the solemn gray-stoned front of the Cambridge County Bank & Loan now sported a thoroughly modern automatic teller, but everything else was there, unchanged and constant. It matched the vivid memories of his boyhood like a photograph that had somehow remained true in the passage of time, retaining its brilliance instead of fading to a disappointing drabness like he had dreaded it would.

Jackson Ridge, Tennessee, had been Jud Simmons's hometown from birth until age twenty-one. He had spent a happy childhood in its peaceful, picturesque setting. But, like many had before, Jud left its comfortable niche of tranquility and had plunged headlong into the urban rat race and a vicious cycle of stress, anxiety, and potential coronaries. In fact, Jud hadn't even thought of stopping in Tennessee on his way back from a business conference in Atlanta. He had been cruising down the interstate when the sign had loomed before him.

NEXT EXIT—JACKSON RIDGE

Nostalgia had gripped him unexpectedly. *I wonder if they still have the Halloween Festival,* he thought. Jud tapped the display monitor on his dashboard, bringing up October's calendar. Yes, this was the weekend it was always scheduled. A moment later, he had turned off the exit, driving down the two-lane rural road, across the old bridge, until he was finally there.

Jud cruised slowly past Chapman's Feed CO-OP and the

low brick building of Jackson Ridge Elementary, marveling at the sameness of it all. He drove along the shop-lined street until he reached the grassy expanse of town square with its ancient oaks, two-story courthouse, and tarnished bronze statue of the Reverend Caleb Jackson, the Lutheran minister who had founded the town in the early 1700s.

The main thoroughfare was unusually quiet, even for a small town, but the sidewalks were lined with cars as far as the eye could see. Jud was lucky to find an empty parking space directly in front of the courthouse. Other than the Halloween Festival, there was one other point of interest that he was most anxious to see again. As he cut his engine, he sat and wondered if *it* was still there.

But of course, it was. It had always been there and always would be.

He left his rental car—a Ford Fusion—and walked to the eastern end of the grassy courtyard, enjoying the crispness of the autumn afternoon. He approached a wide slab of smooth stone and mortar that lay beneath a state historical marker.

The old cistern... there as it had been since the founding of Jackson Ridge in 1733. It had been no more than a simple underground reservoir that had collected rainwater for the few residents when the little town was no more than a trading post for those settlers brave enough to venture into the wilderness south of Virginia.

Jud walked around the vast slab of stone. The cistern... a source of legend and fantasy for young and old alike, a thing of mystery. SEALED IN THE YEAR OF OUR LORD—1765 was chiseled into the great, flat lid that the townsfolk had, for some unknown reason, secured over the pit of the well long ago. Everyone had their favorite stories for exactly why the cistern had been sealed. Some said it had been covered when a typhoid epidemic poisoned the town's water supply, while others claimed that bodies were buried there—the remains of a French trapper and his nine Indian wives, violators of the Reverend Jackson's strict moral code. Almost every kid in town was sure that buried treasure had been stashed there—precious jewels and golden doubloons as big around as the face of Grandpa's pocket watch.

As Jud finished reading the historical marker and looked down at the gray expanse of ancient stone, he was shocked to find that, during his long absence, a long fissure had split the heavy lid. The crack was a good two feet across. Musky darkness gaped from the shadowy depths within. He felt a sinking disappointment grip his heart as he crouched to examine it better. "Now what the hell happened here?" he muttered.

"Joe Bob Tucker got drunk the summer before last," came a child's voice from behind him. "Ran his four-wheel-drive up onto the grass and hit the thing a good lick. They tossed him in the county jail for a whole month just for putting that crack down the middle... I guess because it was a historical thing and all."

Jud turned and regarded the boy. He must have been around nine or ten, a short fellow in faded overalls, a striped T-shirt, and worn sneakers. He was a cute kid, all freckles and bright red hair. From the drabness and ill-fit of his clothing, Jud figured the boy must belong to one of the poor families who had always lived on Esterbrook Road, another unchanging constant in the little hamlet of Jackson Ridge.

"Joe Bob Tucker did you say?" Jud grinned in fond remembrance. "I went to school with a Joe Bob Tucker... kind of lanky fella with buckteeth and a scar across the bridge of his nose?"

The boy nodded. "Yep, that's him all right." He studied the stranger with interest. "So, you were from around here once, mister?"

Jud walked over and extended his hand. "Yeah, a long time ago. My name is Jud Simmons. I live in Chicago now. And what is your name?"

The boy took his hand proudly, delighted to be shaking with a real grown-up. "Name's Calvin... but everyone just calls me Chigger."

Jud laughed good naturedly. "Well, it's mighty nice meeting you, Chigger."

The youngster beamed. "Same here."

The businessman cast his eyes along the street he had just traveled. "You know, I don't believe I've seen a single person since I drove into town. Where is everybody?"

"They're all down at the fairgrounds, mister." Chigger pointed to a colorful poster in a storefront window that proclaimed JACKSON RIDGE HALLOWEEN FESTIVAL / OCTOBER 29-31.

Well, of course they are, he thought. *That's what I came here for, wasn't it?*

For the first time since his arrival, Jud heard sounds drifting over the wooded rise beyond the courthouse. The peppy notes of a circus calliope, the thunder, rattle, and roar of the roller coaster, the steady hum of voices and loud pitches of the barkers on the midway.

"So how come you're not over there joining in the fun?"

Chigger's smile faded. He stared down at his scuffed sneakers in shame. "On account I ain't got no money."

Jud frowned. "Not even enough for the festival?"

"I ain't got *nothing!* Papa says he can't afford to give me an allowance like the other kids, so I can't go." Then with a sudden burst of enthusiasm, he raised his eyes hopefully. "That is, unless *you* treat me!"

Jud couldn't help but grin. "Well, I wasn't planning on staying very long..."

Chigger was suddenly tugging at his hand. "Come on, mister... *please*? We'll have a real good time. There are all kinds of neat things going on down there. Mayor Templeton is judging the jack-o'-lantern carving contest, there's gonna be a tractor pull, and after dark the fire department is having a big firework show. Come on, will you, mister? Please?"

Jud knew there was no need in arguing. "Sure, Chigger, let's do that festival up right!"

He took the boy's small hand and, together, they climbed the rise that overlooked the fairground. They were greeted by the sights, sounds, and smells of Jackson Ridge's annual Halloween Festival. Swapping boyish grins of anticipation, man and child descended into the swirling activity of breakneck carnival rides and colorful sideshow tents.

As afternoon passed into evening and the evening into night, Jud and Chigger had the time of their lives. They rode all the hair-raising rides, played all the midway games, and gorged themselves on junk food.

But, as the sun went down, Jud began to feel a little uneasy, despite the excitement of the festivities. It was the people who milled around them that conjured the sensation that something was basically wrong. He found himself noticing their faces. Instead of the cheerfulness and joviality that should have been there, he witnessed only tension and underlying fear. But why? He could not understand why they would feel such a way in such a festive place. He recognized a few folks from his distant past and tried talking to them, but they merely nodded and moved on or did not acknowledge him at all.

And there were other things, too, like the vendor at the concession stand. Jud had been in the process of buying himself and Chigger a foot-long hotdog and an orange soda, when he glanced up and saw—or *thought* he saw—the vendor's face change slightly. One moment the man appeared normal enough, pudgy and middle-aged, and then the next his features seemed to be creased by some horrid torment, the flesh seared and blistered as if by some great heat. Then, abruptly, the puzzling sight shifted back into reality, returning the man to his former appearance.

"What's the matter, mister?" Chigger asked.

"Nothing," Jud told him. "Nothing at all." But there had been something and, from Chigger's sly grin, he gathered that the boy was somehow privy to it also.

They continued on down the bustling midway decorated with black and orange streamers, cardboard skeletons, and grinning jack-o'-lanterns. As everyone began to prepare for the big fireworks display, Jud's suspicions grew stronger. His apprehension came to a head when Chigger wandered from him for a moment to watch a parade of witches, zombies, and cavorting clowns, some riding unicycles, while others sprayed the crowd with seltzer bottles. Jud was standing beside a tent, when a woman's hand took his arm and drew him into the privacy of the fortune teller's booth. The gypsy who confronted him stared at him with the same expression of anxiety. "You must leave this place now," she warned gravely, "while you still have the opportunity to do so."

"But why?" asked Jud. Instead of being irritated at her

rudeness, he regarded her with an interest born of creeping dread. "What could there possibly be here that could cause me harm?"

The fortune teller's fearful eyes stared out the open door-way. "The boy... the one called Chigger. He is not what he appears to be."

"Don't be silly!" said Jud. "He's just a little kid." He turned and glanced absently out at the midway.

The dancing characters of the Halloween parade were gone. In their place was a procession of naked humanity, writhing and wailing as they ran a gauntlet of hot coals and broken glass.

Jud turned back to the gypsy, his eyes questioning, then again looked outside. The parade participants were back, waving and tossing handfuls of trick-or-treat candy to the crowd.

"I do not have time to explain," said the woman, pushing him toward the rear of the tent. "Just go. Get back to town as fast as you can, get in your car, and drive as far from this place as possible. And never return."

Jud was about to protest when Chigger's voice came from out on the midway. "Mister? Mister, where'd you go?"

Jud almost answered, but caught himself before he could make that fatal mistake. There was something peculiar about that youthful voice, some dark intent hidden beneath the inno-cence and boyish charm. For one fleeting second, Chigger's small form flickered like the waves of a desert mirage, giving a subliminal hint of some awful presence in his place. Something ominous and beyond human comprehension.

"Quickly, through the back way. You haven't got much time!" Without hesitation, Jud took the fortune teller's advice, ducking through a flap in the canvas wall and making his way swiftly along the back lot of the carnival grounds. He ignored little Chigger's inquisitive calls and made it to the wooded rise undiscovered. His heart pounding, Jud topped the knoll just as the first of the fireworks shot skyward, filling the starry night with bursts of heavenly brilliance.

He looked back down at that swirling maelstrom of shows and rides and fun and felt as if he had just been had. *You're noth-ing but a damned fool, Jud Simmons!* he told himself. *You're just*

*letting your imagination run away with you. There's nothing wrong...
not with this place, not with these people, and certainly not with sweet,
little Chigger!*

He was just about to go back down and rejoin his little
friend, when he happened to glance over his shoulder at the
town behind him. Jud's panic flared anew and he leapt down
the steep rise, running toward the collection of quaint buildings
that he had lived among so many years before.

In the eerie light of the skyward explosions, Jud witnessed
what truly existed before him. The town of Jackson Ridge was
in shambles. The picturesque storefronts were now dilapidated
and decayed, their windows hanging in jagged shards. The
paved streets were littered with debris and fissured with deep
cracks. The few vehicles that stood on the street were no more
than rusted hulls, while the grass of the square was scorched an
ugly brownish-black.

Jud felt as if he might pass out. *This can't be for real,* he
thought, although he knew it was. Then he heard a voice call
out from behind him, from the top of the wooded rise. It was
the voice of little Chigger... but, then again, it was also the rum-
bling voice of something that could not possibly possess the
soul of an innocent nine-year-old boy.

"Hey, mister!" it thundered, the tone hitting highs and lows
virtually impossible for the human voice to manage. "Where do
you think you're going? Come back, will you? Do you hear me?
I said... COME BACK!"

Jud Simmons almost turned around and, if he had, would
have surely been lost right then and there. He stood stone still
for an endless moment, acutely aware of something coming
down the rise toward him. Something very *big,* something very
evil. A fetid heat prickled the nape of his neck and the sulfurous
stench of brimstone and burnt flesh assaulted his nostrils. Jud
knew that if he turned to face the thing, its appearance, perhaps
even its very presence, would surely drive him insane. Resisting
the overwhelming urge to commit mental suicide, Jud began to
run as fast as possible up the cluttered avenue of Main Street for
the town square and his car.

A hoarse roar shook the air around him, nearly shattering

his eardrums. "WHERE ARE YOU GOING, MISTER? DON'T
YOU WANNA GO BACK TO THE FESTIVAL? EVERYONE'S
WAITING FOR YOU... CAN'T YOU HEAR THEM?"

Yes, he could hear the sounds coming from over the rise,
but it was no longer the toot of the calliope or the excited voices
of the crowd. The awful screams of tormented souls drilled
through the night air, enhanced by the crackling of flames and
the explosive dishevel of wholesale Armageddon. It was the
sound of an agonizing Hell on earth.

As he ran past the battered shops and stores, a strange thing
happened. The town began to *shift*. Brief flashes of normal-
ity replaced the devastation. Ben Flanders was giving Charlie
Walsh a haircut in the big window of the barber shop, the
elderly Stokes brothers were playing checkers outside the hard-
ware store, and a teenager in a Future Farmers jacket was selling Grit papers in front of the post office. Then, just as swiftly
as it had appeared, the deceptive camouflage returned to death
and destruction. The clever and well-maintained illusion that
had been conjured for the benefit of those outsiders who happened to visit Jackson Ridge from day to day abruptly bled back
into grim reality.

Jud cut across the eastern side of the square for his car. *God,
oh dear God in Heaven, let me make it!* But what if he *did* make it to
the Fusion? Would it make any difference?

He now saw the rusted wreck of Joe Bob's 4x4 pickup truck
where it hadn't been before, hanging on the lip of the square, its
front bumper stuck in the split stone of the cistern. It looked as
though the windshield had imploded from some terrible force.
Jud suddenly knew that his car would be no protection whatsoever from the thing that pursued him.

"COME ON BACK, MISTER! YOU SAID YOU'D TREAT ME
TO THE FESTIVAL. YOU PROMISED YOU WOULD!" The horrid voice was strangely infantile, yet as old as time itself. And
there was an underlying evil, a gleeful cruelty in every syllable
it spoke. Whatever dark realm the demon had originated from,
its very presence exuded a foul sense of utter depravity that
made Satan's threat seem pale in comparison.

The thing was gaining on him. He could hear its approach,

like a thousand pounding feet in hot pursuit, growing ever nearer. *It's going to catch me,* Jud thought wildly. *It's going to grab hold of me and... what? What in heaven's name will it do to me then?* He could sense the thing's vast bulk as it shifted to his right. It was heading toward the car, trying to cut him off! Jud's legs felt like rubber. He knew he couldn't possibly beat it to the car. Abruptly, a crazy idea crossed his desperate mind and he acted on it. He veered sharply to the left, past the historical marker, and squeezed through the gaping crack in the lid of the cistern.

Cool darkness met him, as well as empty air. He fell for what seemed to be an eternity, before hitting the smooth hardness of the reservoir floor. Jud lay there for a long, silent moment, the breath knocked completely from his lungs. Even after regaining his senses, he stayed put, staring up at the fissure eight feet overhead. He awaited the inevitable, but it did not come. It appeared as though the demon was somewhat reluctant to enter the place that had entombed it for over two centuries.

Moments passed. Jud sat up, his eyes still glued to that jagged black slit with its sparkling backdrop of firework-filled sky. When the ogre finally appeared, Jud was not at all surprised to see the innocent, freckled face of the boy staring down at him.

"Come on, mister," begged little Chigger. "Don't be an Indian giver. You said we were gonna do the festival up right. We can still have loads of fun, you'll see. We'll eat buttered popcorn and those big salty pretzels, and we'll carve pumpkins and bob for apples, and see the freak show and we'll ride the Wild Mouse and the Tilt-a-Twirl and..."

Jud listened to the innocent voice for a long time, reeling off the simple pleasures of the Halloween Festival. He could even hear the music and the crowd again, could smell the rich fragrance of roasted peanuts and sawdust. He wanted to go back, he truly did, but he knew what awaited him if he dared succumb.

The crackle of hellfire would mask the pops of the firing range, the pungency of cooked flesh would overshadow the sticky sweet smell of cotton candy, and his screams would join those of the damned.

PRETTY LITTLE LANTERNS

Sheriff Jonah Townshend hated Halloween.

More than any other time of year, the last couple of weeks in the month of October filled him with a terrible sense of uneasiness and impending dread.

For that was the time that the jack-o'-lanterns appeared.

The ones that weren't pumpkins.

It had begun three years ago. In 1925, there had been one. A precocious, teenaged girl named Sally Toller had come up missing the night before Halloween, during a walk home from a showing of *The Lost World* at the Sublime Theater in the rural Tennessee town of Green Hollow. The following night, she showed up… or, at least, *part* of her did. Her lovely, blond head had been hollowed out—brain, eyes, the sinuses, the tissues of her inner mouth and tongue, all discarded—and a lit candle placed within her empty skull. A group of trick-or-treating youngsters saw it first and had fled, screaming. Poor Sally's body had never been found.

In 1926, there were two: the Whittaker Sisters, Maude and Marge. The spinsters, well into their seventies, had suffered a similar fate. Their heads graced the front windows of their little, clapboard house on Brighton Avenue. This time, a number of their upper and lower teeth had been removed, giving them the uneven grins of a traditional jack-o'-lantern. Their bodies were discovered in their beds… still dressed in their nightgowns with patchwork quilts pulled up snuggly around the stubs of their wrinkled necks.

1927 had been a particularly bad year for the victims of Doctor Jack… a name given to the killer by the *Green Hollow Gazette*. Four human lanterns had been discovered within a ten-mile radius. One had been Harvey Purdue at the filling station just past the city limits, two had been a young married couple, Frank and Amy Childress, and the fourth was, Janet McClain, the wife of the town mayor. Mayor McClain had returned home late the night before Halloween after a long council meeting to find Janet's head impaled on the pickets of the front gate, her face pale and slack, an awful pinkish glow emanating from her empty eye sockets, nostrils, and mutilated mouth. The McClain children slept peacefully upstairs, unaware that anything had happened to their mother.

Sheriff Townshend had never found a shred of evidence or any clues to help him track down the one responsible. The state police had even helped with the investigation, but all their law enforcement savvy and knowledge had led them nowhere.

Absolutely no one in the little mountain town of Green Hollow, or Sevier County for that matter, had any idea who could have been deranged and evil enough to perform the grisly murders and constructed the hideous jack-o'-lanterns.

No one, that was, except the town librarian, Miss Gladys Willoughby.

Sheriff Townshend was sitting in a booth at the Anytime Café, nursing a cup of coffee, when she slid into the seat across from him. The lawman lifted his cup and hid a frown with a long sip. *What the hell is she up to now,* he wondered. Miss Gladys was a notorious busybody and firm believer in conspiracies, the stranger and more outrageous the better.

Before he could say good morning, she launched into her spiel, eyes bright and excited, and a mischievous grin on her lean face. "Jonah! I know who it is!"

"What are you talking about, Miss Gladys?"

"Why, Doctor Jack, of course!"

Jonah swallowed another sip of coffee. "Now, why did you have to mention *him* this early in the morning?"

"Because we're going to solve it this year!" she declared. "We're going to bag Ol' Jack and bring him to justice."

"Okay, Miss Gladys... who is it this time? Last year it was the Bell Witch and the year before that the Skunk Ape... whatever the hell a skunk ape is."

"No, no, no! All false leads. I've been doing some serious investigating this year, with help from my sister, Beatrice."

"The one who lives overseas?"

"Yes!" said Gladys. "In London. She moved to England after finishing school, because of her love of Arthur Conan Doyle's Sherlock Holmes. She has always wanted to be an amateur detective."

Sort of like you, he thought to himself. "So, what would Beatrice know about what's happening here in Green Hollow?"

"Well," Gladys began, rubbing her bony hands together, "she has been dating a man who works at Scotland Yard... it's sort of like our Federal Bureau of Investigation, you know, only British. He's an older gentleman who's worked there for nearly fifty years. A police photographer!"

Jonah glanced at the clock that hung over the mirror behind the eating counter. "Miss Gladys, I've got to be getting to the office..."

"Just be patient, Jonah... I'm getting to the point."

Please, thought the sheriff, completely impatient. *Please! Get to the damn point!*

"Anyway, Beatrice has been sending me research materials. Old newspapers and photographs that her beau developed using some of the original negatives from the crime investigation."

"Crime investigation of *what*?"

"Not *what*, Jonah, but *who*!" The skinny librarian glanced around the café, leaned forward, and lowered her voice. "None other than Leather Apron. Old Spring-heel Jack himself!"

"Aw, Miss Gladys... you don't mean..."

"Yes! Doctor Jack is none other than Jack the Ripper!"

Jonah couldn't help but groan. "You mean that fellow that carved up all those women?"

"Prostitutes!" hissed Gladys distastefully. "Ladies of the evening."

"Yeah, but that was forty years ago. If the Ripper were in his thirties or forties back then, he'd be an old man right now. In his seventies or eighties, at least. And, frankly, I don't know any men that age in Sevier County that weren't born and bred here in Tennessee."

"Oh, but there is!" she said. Her eyes were excited, like a child about to ride the carrousel for the first time. "Nigel Whitehall." Jonah stared at her for a long moment. "The dentist? Now, Miss Gladys, be reasonable. That old man is the kindest, most harmless man around these parts."

"Yes... he very well *seems* to be," agreed Gladys. "But consider this. He's British, he only came to this community four years ago—after old Doc Harvey died of mysterious circumstances—and his name, well, that's the kicker."

"What about his name?"

She stared at Jonah as if he were twelve kinds of ignorant. "Whitehall? It's got to be a sly alteration of Whitechapel... the Ripper's killing ground! Just him coming here, using that name, means he's arrogant and overconfident. He's taunting us... daring us to figure out who he really is."

Sheriff Townshend stood up and put his hat on his head, ready to get out of there. "Miss Gladys... please do me a favor. Keep your suspicions and opinions to yourself, and leave that nice, old man alone. Everyone loves Dr. Whitehall. My kids adore him... and they hate going to the dentist."

The librarian looked hurt and offended. "Well, I was only trying to help, Sheriff. I thought you could use all the assistance you could get, what with Doctor Jack leaving heads all over the county every October since '25. I'm not an airheaded gossip like most of the women in this town. I've got college schooling. I've got some smarts in my noggin."

Jonah felt sort of bad about putting her off the way he had. "Yes, you do, Miss Gladys, and I appreciate your input. You're right... I can use all the help I can get to solve these crimes."

The librarian nodded her graying head curtly. "You see! I'm on the right track. If you want to see the materials and photographs that Beatrice sent me, just come on over to the library and they're yours for the taking. And, if you feel you're in need of my expertise, I'll be more than happy to take the oath and honor the badge that goes with it."

Jonah had to lock up his face muscles to keep from cracking a big grin. If he deputized a feisty, old spinster librarian, he would be the laughingstock of the entire county. "If I feel that it comes to that, Miss Gladys, I'll certainly take it under consideration."

Miss Gladys smiled smugly, then left the booth and marched out the front door, heading down the street toward the library.

Jonah Townshend sighed and took one last sip of his coffee. It was lukewarm and bitter.

"Well," said Pamela, the waitress behind the counter.

"Well, what?"

"Are you going to take that shriveled old bookworm up on her offer and swear her in?"

Jonah was aggravated. "You heard all that?"

Pamela laughed. "Who couldn't for a quarter mile? She's got a voice that carries like a Winchester rifle at a turkey shoot."

"That she does." Jonas appealed to the waitress's kind heart. "Could you see fit to keep this under your hat, Pam? Folks are giving me enough grief already, without adding Deputy Gladys to my list of woes."

"I'm on your side, Sheriff. That old biddy thinks she's twice as smart as anyone else in town, which rubs me and a lot of folks the wrong way. Besides, she's a few bricks shy of a full load. Folks know that, too."

Jonah nodded his thanks, left her a dime tip on the counter, and headed for his office.

On his way, half-a-dozen citizens stopped and asked him about Doctor Jack, if he had any earthly idea who the culprit was, and what was Jonah's chances of catching him before Halloween rolled around. Jonah had nothing new to tell them. Most seemed a little peeved and dissatisfied with the job he was doing... or, in their opinion, *wasn't* doing.

Lord, he prayed, *please get me through the end of October without another one of those damned pumpkin heads showing up.*

But, unfortunately, if the Almighty was listening, He turned a deaf ear to the sheriff's pleas.

The first one of that Halloween season showed up the following night.

Jonah was at home having supper with his family—it was

white beans and cornbread night—when the phone on the wall rang. He glanced at his wife, Millicent, who gave him a questioning look. Both knew that no one called the house unless it was an absolute emergency.

The sheriff found that the town operator, Flossie Smith, had patched the caller straight through, which wasn't a good sign. Flossie usually liked to talk a spell before she finished the connection. Jonah brought the receiver to his ear and moved closer to the mouthpiece. "Hello? This is Sheriff Townshend speaking."

A man's frantic voice sounded through a crackle of static. The fellow sucked air heavily, as if fighting to catch his breath. Also, he had a thick lisp. Jonah knew immediately who it was.

"Sheriff... this here's Andy Moore." The man, who Jonah knew to be at least three hundred and fifty pounds, maybe more, began to wheeze loudly.

"Just take a couple of deep breaths, Andy, and tell me what's going on."

The man did as the sheriff suggested and gained his composure. "Sheriff... I'm down here at the Double Dice... first one here... found the door open, so I just walked in."

Jonah knew the place well. It was a roadhouse several miles west of town, out on the state highway. He had been there many a time to break up barroom brawls, bust up an unruly game of poker or craps, or drive some drunken farmer home to his wife.

"And what did you—?"

"It was one of *them!*" moaned Andy. "One of those jack-o'-lanterns! Carved by the Devil himself! Oh... God... it was Stu Jenkins, Sheriff!"

Stu was the proprietor and bartender of the Double Dice. "I'm on my way," he told the man. "Don't touch anything!"

"Touch anything? I'm sure not gonna touch that damn fool thing! I don't even want to look at it!"

Jonah hung up the phone, went to the hall closet, and took his gun belt off the hook inside of the door. He buckled and adjusted the holster on his way out.

Millicent caught him on the front porch, out of earshot of the kids. "It's another one, isn't it?"

He turned and regarded his wife. Curly blond and buxom...

every bit as beautiful as that night when he first met her at the Sevier County Fair fourteen years ago. "Yeah... the first one. Hopefully the last." Even as he said it, Jonah knew that was nothing more than wishful thinking.

They reached out, held one another's hand for a couple of seconds, then let go. No time for a kiss. "I'll be back directly," he promised.

She nodded and said nothing more. Just watched, arms crossed, as he ran down the front walk to his '26 Packard. He jumped in, cranked the starter, and—making a sharp U-turn in the street—headed for the west side of town.

When he got to the Double Dice, Jonah found Andy Moore sitting by the entrance door, his back to the wall. He had vomited on himself. Puke ran down the front of his flannel shirt and the bib of his overalls, pooling in his ample lap. His big, moon-round face was pale as a slug and sweaty.

Jonah crouched next to the man and laid a hand on his thick shoulder. "You alright, Andy?"

"I... I sicked up on myself," the man muttered. His lips were coated with bile and bits of food.

"Can you show me where—?"

Andy's eyes widened. "Shit no, I ain't going back in there! Don't think I'll ever set foot in this joint again! No drink or hand of cards is worth what I laid eyes on. No sir!"

The sheriff patted the man's shoulder. He stood, unsnapped the retaining strap on his holster and withdrew his sidearm... a 1917 Smith & Wesson .45 revolver.

There were no lights on inside the roadhouse. The only glow came from the center of the long mahogany wood bar. As Jonah moved nearer, he felt bile rise into his own throat and quickly choked it back down.

"Good God Almighty!" was all that he could manage to say.

Stu Jenkins's decapitated head was impaled on a large bottle of whiskey. The neck of the bottle had been rammed up through the channel of Stu's open throat and a wax candle stuck into the vessel's mouth and lit. It flickered and guttered inside the man's empty skull, a warm pinkish-yellow glow emanating from the open eye sockets, the channels of the nostrils, and the slack-jawed mouth. A number of teeth had been forcefully yanked from the gums and discarded, leaving a jagged, haphazard grin on the makeshift jack-o'-lantern. Even as he stared at the bottle-impaled head of Stu Jenkins, he couldn't help but notice the bartender's tip jar sitting on the bar near the cash register. It was half full of blood and, floating within its thickening contents, was Stu's iron-gray eyes and several of his missing teeth.

The following afternoon, a coroner from the state lab came down and took a look at it.

"I'll be damned if this isn't a pretty piece of work," said the doctor, whose name was Wallace. There was a peculiar look on his whiskered face—part admiration, part revulsion.

"What can you tell me about it?" Jonah asked him.

Wallace walked around the head, which was sitting, alone, on a steel gurney at the local funeral home. "Well... whoever did it knew what they were doing. I mean, there was a lot of thought and skill involved. It wasn't done by a layman. Whoever killed this man had a thorough knowledge of anatomy."

Jonah simply stood there silently and let the coroner perform his examination. "He used an instrument of some kind to remove the cap of the skull... a bone saw, more than likely. It was done with precision and a steady hand. The cut started at the frontal bone, continued past the coronal suture, then completely through the parietal bone. The brain, which you discovered in a spittoon, was undamaged, so the murderer was extremely meticulous in his work. I would even hazard to say that, more than likely, Mr. Jenkins was still alive when this took place.

"After the cerebral cortex, cerebellum, and the stem of the medulla oblongata were removed, the killer began cleaning the inside of the skull, much the way we would pull the guts and refuse from a pumpkin. He cut away the tissues of the nasal cavity... the superior, middle, and inferior turbinate, as well as the plate of the upper palate, the tongue, and the linings of the inner mouth and the throat. After that, the killer shattered the cups of the occipital bone and extracted the eyes, taking hold of the optic nerve and pulling them through the skull from the rear of the sockets. After that, he had an empty chamber in which to make his gruesome Halloween decoration. He shoved the neck of the liquor bottle up through the channel of the esophagus— or what was left of it following the decapitation—to be used as a stand for the head and a receptacle for the candle."

"Damn," said Jonah. "Someone would have to be a madman to do something like this."

"Yes," agreed Wallace, "but a very cold and calculating madman. It wasn't the wild, frenzied act of your run-of-the-mill lunatic... not the kind that jabbers to himself and pisses his pants. No, this man was a special kind of crazy... a killing machine with no inhibition or respect for the sanctity of life. And I'd say he had been significantly schooled in the inner workings of the human body."

"What are you saying, Mr. Wallace?"

The coroner stepped back and regarded the altered head of Stu Jenkins. "What I'm saying, Sheriff Townshend, that whoever did this was no amateur. I'd even go so far as say he might be a doctor or even a surgeon... a methodical professional of tremendous skill and nerve."

The following afternoon, Jonas took his son, Matthew, to see the dentist.

The ten-year-old had been climbing a tree at school when he fell and smacked his mouth on a limb coming down. The fall had knocked the wind out of Matthew, blooded his lips, and chipped his left front tooth.

"Can you do anything to fix it, Doc?" the sheriff asked.

Nigel Whitehall tenderly pulled back the boy's injured lips and examined the tooth in question. "Short of pulling it, truthfully, no," said the tall, lean man with the snow-white hair and handlebar mustache. "I'm afraid young, master Matthew will have to live with an uneven grin upon his countenance from now on."

"Aw, shucks!" mumbled the boy around the dentist's probing fingers.

"I wouldn't fret, Matthew," said the elderly man, directing a wink in his father's direction. "Such an abnormality is like a scar of battle. It gives a man character... separates him from the mundane and the ordinary."

"So," said Jonah, "can you file it down or something? It looks sort of sharp. I don't want the boy to cut his lips on it. They're already battered and bruised enough from that tree limb."

"I most certainly can, Constable," assured Whitehall. He reached over and took a small, thin file with a wooden handle from a tray of dentistry tools. The dentist rolled an elevated stool to the side of the adjustable chair and took a seat. Then he leaned forward with the file in hand. "Now, Matthew, this isn't going to hurt, but it may make you shudder or flinch. Not because of pain, but because the sound of it will make your skin crawl... like fingernails on the blackboard at school."

Matthew laughed, then grew still as the old man began to smooth the jagged tooth down.

Jonah watched with interest as the dentist worked. "You have a steady hand, Doc," he said.

A thin grin crossed Whitehall's wrinkled face. "Well, I should... I was a surgeon for nearly fifty years."

The sheriff's heart skipped a beat, but he didn't let it show. "Oh, really? Here in America?"

"Goodness, no!" replied Whitehall with a chuckle. "London. I learned my trade at Barts and, following medical school, plied my trade at St. Mary's Hospital on Praed Street. And, not to be boastful, but I was the most promising and skilled surgeon on the premises."

Watching the man's long, nimble hands working skillfully, with precision and accuracy, so close to his son's mouth... his head... seemed to fill Jonah with an odd sense of unease. "So, Doc... why did you give up surgery and become a dentist?"

"Oh, there were several reasons," said Whitehall absently, his attention focused on the broken tooth. "I suppose I grew tired of spending most of my time elbows-deep in someone's chest or abdomen. The human body is a wondrous device, as well-timed and dependable as a Swiss timepiece. But it is bloody messy when you're trying to remove a stubborn tumor or rearrange the dislodged organs of a hernia to their former position. After a while, you tend to grow sick of seeing the inside of humanity. I prefer constructing a beautiful smile than rummaging around in someone's bowels and intestines."

"Yeech!" mumbled Matthew.

"Hold still, young man," advised the dentist, "or else I'll end up filing down that boyish tongue of yours."

"And that was all there was to it?" asked Jonah. "You simply grew tired of being a surgeon."

"Well, there was another reason," said Whitehall. "The death of my dear wife, Daphne." The elderly man's face seemed to tense and his eyes grew unfocused for a moment, as though staring at something far from the office they now sat in. "She was with child... our first child. Daphne went into labor while I was away at a medical conference in Paris. When the baby became lodged in the birth canal, a surgeon was called in. A very inexperienced and arrogant young doctor named Dawson. If I had been there, I would have performed a Cesarean section on my wife and liberated the child. But, no, not Dawson. He practically gutted poor Daphne... made an incision from beneath her sternum, clear to her pubic bone. After that, she bled to death very quickly. She died on the operating table... along with the child... my daughter."

"Doctor Whitehall," Jonah said softly. Drawing the elderly man's attention, he nodded quietly toward his son, whose eyes were wide with fascination.

"Oh, I do apologize, Constable," said Whitehall regretfully. "I didn't mean to ramble on so... and with such ill restraint. I certainly hope that I didn't frighten the lad with my grisly talk."

"He'll be okay," said the sheriff. "He's always dwelling on gruesome things, especially around Halloween."

Whitehall laughed and, finished with his task, placed the file back on the steel tray of instruments. "All Hallows' Eve! Pagan festival of the Druids. A celebration of death. Leave it to you yanks to turn it into a fun night for costumes and candy. So, Master Matthew... what shall you be this year?"

"A cowboy!" the boy said with a big grin. "Tom Mix!"

"And young Mistress Vickie?"

"A witch! What else would she be?"

"Matt!" his father scolded with a warning look.

That made Nigel Whitehall laugh even harder. "Why don't you run along and ask Mrs. Pendleton to let you select a little something from the prize box."

"Wow!" said the boy, leaping out of the dentist chair. "Thanks a bunch, Dr. Whitehall!"

As the boy ran through the doorway into the outer office, Whitehall eyed Jonah curiously. "Are you alright, Constable? You seemed a bit perturbed."

"I reckon it's all this business with these killings," he said. To tell the truth, that was most of the reason, but not all of it. "These damn jack-o'-lanterns."

"Oh, yes" said Whitehall grimly. "The infamous Doctor Jack. A fellow like that must possess an extremely skewed sense of humor... as well as a cold-blooded nature leaning toward sadism."

Jonah debated in his mind, then took a chance. "Like, maybe... Jack the Ripper?"

Nigel Whitehall's bushy white brows lifted sharply. "I must say... I haven't heard that name for quite a while."

The sheriff felt like he was treading on thin ice. "You were there... in London... when it happened, weren't you?"

That distant look shone in the dentist eyes again. "Yes. In '88. Dreadful business. Nasty. Those poor women... and the things he did to them."

Jonah wanted to ask one more question. *He was never caught, was he?* But he didn't. No need to push his luck.

"Well, I'd best get Matthew home," he said. "I've got some patrolling to do before suppertime."

Whitehall seemed to snap out of his funk. "Yes, be ever vigilant, Constable. I wish you much luck at capturing this scoundrel."

"Thanks, Doc," said Jonah and took his leave.

At the reception desk, Matthew was rummaging through the contents of the dentist's prize box... an old White Owl cigar box full of dime store treats and toys.

"Look, Papa! A silver whistle!" He took a large, tin whistle from the box and blew it shrilly.

"Well, you spit in it, now you own it," said his father. "But don't go pestering your mama with it. She's already on edge."

Matthew examined the whistle. "How come?"

"Never you mind. Come on and I'll run you by the house."

Jonah drove his son home and then headed back downtown. Before he reached his office at the courthouse, he pulled over and cut the engine. He just sat there for a while. Thinking.

Finally, he climbed out of the Packard and walked across the street to the library. He walked through tall shelves of books, past the reading area with its oriental carpet and tall, wing-backed chairs, and stepped up to the big, half-circle desk.

Miss Gladys sat there, as she always did, with a vainglorious smile on her narrow, bespectacled face.

"I've been expecting you," she said. She reached beneath the desk, brought out a stack of yellowed newspapers and manila envelopes, and slid them across the counter. "I wouldn't let your children see those. There's some mighty unpleasant things in there… particularly the photographs."

"Thanks, Miss Gladys," he said, tucking them under his arm.

"Oh, and remember…" The librarian raised her right hand and plastered a solemn expression across her wrinkled face.

Not on your life, sister, thought Jonah and headed for his office.

The Thursday evening before Halloween, Jonah came home with two, good-sized pumpkins from Ted Haskell's pumpkin patch a few miles out of town. The kids were excited and anxious to work on them. They ate supper—pork roast, stewed potatoes, and collards—then prepared for the fun. Millicent gathered newspaper for the mess, while Matthew and Vickie debated who would do what. Their father acted as moderator and assigned the tasks. Vickie would draw the faces on the pumpkins and Matthew would do the carving.

While his parents watched, Matthew finished cutting around the crown of the first pumpkin. He pried at the stem until the plug came loose with a moist *pop*. Without hesitation, they boy plunged both hands inside and began to scoop out the stringy guts.

"Papa?"

"Yes, son?"

The boy slung the refuse of the pumpkin onto the newspaper it sat upon and then began picking seeds off his juice-slickened hands. "Do you think Doctor Jack does it like this?"

Jonah looked over a Millicent. His wife shook her pretty head and shrugged, as if saying *he's your son*.

Jonah tried to defuse the question before he fished for too many details and frightened his little sister. "Let's don't go getting too curious. Ain't fitting for a young'un to be thinking of such things."

But the ten-year-old wouldn't leave it alone. "Jimmy Paul at school says he takes the brain out first, then pulls the eyes out from the back, and not pry them out of the sockets from the front."

Jonah studied his six-year-old daughter. Vickie stood there, lead pencil in hand, her eyes as big around as her mother's tea saucers. "Matthew... I believe that's enough."

Apparently, though, it wasn't enough for him. "Then he chisels out the bones of the face from the inside and pulls out the roof of the mouth and tongue. He leaves a few teeth... but takes a few... so it'll really look like a jack-o'-lantern."

Vickie's freckled face grew as pale as baking flour. They could see that she was on the verge of crying. "Mama!"

Millicent stepped in with that calming effect she had on her children. She could soothe a toy-wanting fit at Buford's Five & Dime with a single, gentle look, where it took a good slap or two on the rump for Jonah to end the tantrum. "Vickie... sweetie... don't pay your brother's silly talk any mind. You know how he is... trying to get a rise out of you anytime he can. Now dry up those tears and show him that backbone your mama blessed you with."

With a sniff, the girl stood tall and glared at the brother angrily.

Jonah looked over when his wife cleared her throat. She nodded toward the house. "Okay, you two keep working on those pumpkins," he told his children. "Vickie, you draw those faces real pretty."

"Okay, Daddy," the girl said, back to her cheerful self.

"Matt." He waited until the boy looked him square in the eye. "You keep a steady hold on that knife... and on your tongue. Understand?"

The boy knew his father meant business. "Yes, sir."

Inside the kitchen, Millicent shook her head. "Where did that come from? I know boys his age have an odd interest in things like that... but that was a little much."

"Folks are talking about it all over town, dear," Jonah told her. "It's just natural the kids would get wind of it at school. Half their mothers are busybody gossips. Can't keep their yaps shut for a moment."

Millicent gave him a sly look. "Well, I'm sure not one of them!"

"Of course," he replied. "Whatever you say, dear."

They both shared a laugh at that. Then his wife's face grew serious again. "What Matthew said... is it really like that?"

"*Very* much like that," her husband admitted. "I swear, folks better keep their opinions to themselves... or they might end up on a fence post like those others."

Millicent looked uneasy. "Jonah... do you know who it is?"

"Maybe. I have my suspicions."

She frowned at him and cocked one eyebrow. "Or someone's been feeding them to you. Like maybe Gladys Willoughby? Jonah, you know she's the biggest troublemaker and busybody of them all. Always got some hair-brained conspiracy up her sleeve."

"Now, why would you think—?"

"I know you've been talking to her over at the café," she said flatly. "And I know what about. Folks have ears, you know."

"And a tongue to tell it with."

His wife smirked. "She's been telling everyone it's Jack the Ripper."

"I've been looking at some old newspapers and files that Miss Gladys's sister sent her—"

Millicent's eyes widened. "So, you are in cahoots with her!"

"Nonsense! I'm just studying them... trying to figure out

why a man would get pleasure or reward from cutting folks up like that. The Ripper's victims were all poor, working-class women—some of them whores—but their mutilation was nothing like we've got going on here in Sevier County. His *modus operandi* was nothing like Doctor Jack's."

Millicent shuddered. "All this talk makes me nervous. Whoever's doing this, he may know you're after him. If he knows you're getting too close, he might turn the knife on *you*."

Jonah walked over and gave her a hug. "Don't worry none about me. I'll be careful."

"You'd better... or I'll stick your knobby head on a fence post myself!"

They laughed again, but there was an edge to their humor this time.

Jonah walked to the kitchen window and watched his children as they worked diligently on the pumpkins. *If you're not careful... extremely careful... that's liable to be exactly what happens, too.*

On the Friday night before Halloween, Doctor Jack's second victim lit the darkness of Jefferson Springs Road.

A local farmer, Hud Davidson, had been very vocal about the killings and had declared that, if Doctor Jack came calling at his house, he'd get a couple of barrels of double-aught buckshot for his trouble. Everyone knew that Hud was a blowhard and a big-talker, so they just laughed at his boasting. They didn't laugh any longer when Myrtle Spaulding bicycled home from the late shift at the textile mill and saw Hud's glowing head sitting in the concrete birdbath in his front yard.

This time the state police arrived a half hour after Jonah did. Together, they searched Davidson's farmhouse. The found the farmer's body on the bedroom floor, still dressed in his nightshirt, which was completely soaked with blood. The double-barrel shotgun that Hud had bragged about in town was jammed, to the trigger guard, down the cavity of the esophagus, clear to his stomach.

They were leaving the house, when an officer called from

the side of the house. "We've got a window open on this side and what looks like a very clear thumbprint."

The man in charge, Detective Rawlings, called for someone to bring a fingerprint kit. Jonah watched as the man went to work, applying the dusting powder to the bottom middle pane of glass in the bedroom window. The oval imprint, which was practically invisible before, began to take form as Rawlings gently brushed the fine, black powder, bringing out the swirls and ridges of the print. Satisfied with the application, the detective took a broad piece of lifting tape and gently laid it over the evidence. "You press lightly," Rawlings told the sheriff. "If you press too hard, it'll distort the print and be useless." Soon, he peeled the tape away and, taking a white card from the kit, applied the tape to the paper square. The print was immaculate.

"You think you could do this?" he asked the sheriff.

"Probably," Jonah said. "Why?"

"Because the next time this happens, more than likely me and half the East Tennessee division won't be riding in on white horses. Lately, most of my manpower has been tied up over in Fear County, investigating some ugly business that's been going on."

"I hear it's a mighty bad place," Jonah replied.

Rawlings nodded grimly. "You have no idea."

They walked to the detective's car. Rawlings handed him a duplicate kit from the trunk. "If you see any prints next time, lift them and bring them to us. We'll have a man in the lab compare them. Just be careful and don't smug it."

"I'll sure do that," agreed the sheriff.

"Do you want Wallace to come out and take a look at Davidson's head tomorrow?"

"No need," said Jonah. "Once you see one jack-o'-lantern head, you've seen 'em all."

"Very funny." Detective Rawlings glanced over at his men and lowered his voice. "You watch your back, Townshend. I've seen some crazies, but none that compare to this one. He loves to play with flesh and blood, and he's got balls... and I don't mean the victims'. If you get too close... if he feels you breathing down his neck, he may turn feral and latch into you, like a cornered dog."

Now, where have I heard that before? thought Jonah. "I'll be careful."

"See that you do. There's more to you than these other hick sheriffs I deal with from day to day. You've got backbone and brains. I'd hate to see both of them out in the open... like that poor bastard lying in there with a twelve-gauge shoved down his gullet."

It was nearly two in the morning when they finally finished and left the Davidson farm.

Jonah considered driving home, but he had a lot on his mind. If he had climbed into bed, he would have just tossed and turned, and received an angry grumble and a good kick in the shins from Millicent for his restlessness.

Instead, he went back to town. It was half past the hour when he unlocked his office door, switched on the green-shaded lamp on his desk, and sat down.

He sure could have used a good, strong cup of black coffee at that moment, but there was none to be had. Jonah sat and drummed a pencil on his desk blotter for a few minutes, then reached into a side drawer and brought out the stack of old newspapers and manila envelopes that Gladys Willoughby had given him.

He opened an envelope and took out several black and white photographs. Jonah laid them one beside the other, across his desk. They were awful things to look at– crime scene and autopsy photos of the Ripper's Whitechapel murder spree.

Mary Ann Nichols. Found on Buck's Row. Throat severed by two cuts, one of which went clean down to the neck bone. Lower abdomen ripped clean open by a deep, jagged wound. Several stab wounds to her right side.

Annie Chapman. Discovered at 29 Hanbury Street. Like Nichols, her throat was cut in two places. Abdomen cut entirely open and stomach and small intestines placed upon her left and right shoulders.

The autopsy revealed that her uterus, bladder, and vagina had been removed. The organs had not been found with the body.

Elizabeth Stride. Found in Dutfield's Yard, off Berner Street. The cause of death was a single incision across her neck, which had severed her left carotid artery and trachea. No further mutilation led police to believe that the Ripper had been interrupted during the attack.

Catherine Eddowes. Discovered in Mitre Square in London on the same night as Stride. Throat slashed, abdomen ripped open, intestines slung over her shoulder like Chapman. Left kidney and uterus removed, face badly disfigured. The coroner's postmortem determined that it would have taken at least five minutes to have mutilated Eddowes in such a manner.

Mary Jane Kelly. Lying on a bed in the single room where she lived at 13 Miller's Court, off Dorset Street...

Jonah had looked at the photo only once... but never again. Kelly had been the worst of the five. Her bedroom had been nothing short of a slaughterhouse.

The sheriff sat back in his chair and rubbed his eyes. *What the hell are you doing? This has nothing to do with what's going on in Green Hollow. You're grasping at straws because some old dentist down the street was a surgeon back in England. That old maid librarian has got you spooked with all her talk and this gruesome stuff she's given you.*

Absently, he reached out and grabbed one the London newspapers, a yellow-paged copy of *The Daily Telegraph*. It was dated December 17, 1888.

He flipped through it, but found little of interest. A few articles about the Ripper, mostly stating that his reign of terror had ended in November and there had been no further murders attributed to him. Jonah was nearing the classified advertisements in the back, when a small article caught his eye.

LONDON SURGEON FOUND SLAIN

A prominent surgeon of St. Mary's Hospital was found deceased last Tuesday evening in his flat at 322 Eastbourne Terrace in Paddington. Everett Martin Dawson, who had been a general surgeon at St. Mary's for seven years, had not reported for his morning shift earlier that day. Concerned acquaintances, curious of his whereabouts, went to Eastbourne Terrace and discovered the front door of the flat ajar. The body of Dawson was found on the floor of the parlor, a victim of foul play. The doctor's body had been hideously mutilated.

Upon leaving the flat to summon the police, Dawson's acquaintances detected the odor of burning flesh and hair, and looked up to see their friend's decapitated head wedged into the cage of a nearby streetlamp. Dawson's skull had been hollowed out and impaled on the mantle of the lamp's gas burners...

Jonah Townshend let the newspaper fall from his hands, onto the desk before him. Words echoed in his head... an innocent conversation from a couple of days ago.

When the baby became lodged in the birth canal, a surgeon was called in. A very inexperienced and arrogant young doctor named Dawson.

"Well, I'll be damned," he said, jumping up out of his chair.

Jonah paced the floor of his office, thoughts racing in his head. Finally, he knew what he must do. He reached into a desk drawer and brought out a large key ring– spare keys of all the stores and offices along Green Hollow's main street. As sheriff, the shopkeepers and professionals of town had entrusted him with access to their businesses, in the event of an emergency.

He found the one he needed in the very middle... a brass key with the number 83 engraved in the metal.

Jonah took it, a flashlight, and the fingerprint kit, then left the office. Downstairs, he left the courthouse, crossed the street, and walked two blocks down to a small, brick-front business. A sign next to the door read NIGEL J. WHITEHALL, DDS.

The sheriff looked around, but there was no one in sight. Everyone in town and the surrounding countryside was asleep at three o'clock in the morning. He slipped the brass key in the lock and opened the door.

Once inside, he snapped on the flashlight. A pale glow illuminated the waiting room and the window where the receptionist always sat. Jonah shifted the fingerprint kit to beneath his armpit and unfastened the retaining strap on his holster. His heart beat heavy and hard, like a jackhammer.

He entered the doorway next to the office and found himself in Whitehall's examination room. There was the adjustable dentist chair, the porcelain spit sink, a tall white cabinet with glass panes, and a rolling table with the stainless-steel instrument tray. In the glow of the flashlight, Jonah examined the picks, dental pliers, and other tools of the dentist trade. The file with the wooden handle caught his eyes. *Now I know there's a print on that thing,* he thought. *Hopefully a good one.*

The sheriff laid the flashlight and the fingerprint kit on the seat of the dentist chair. He was about to open the little wooden box and get to work, when the overhead light suddenly blazed to life.

Alarmed, he whirled and tried to see who was behind him, his eyes slowly adjusting to the brightness.

"Time to have a much-needed chat, Constable," said Nigel Whitehall.

The elderly man drew a small gun from his pocket. It was a derringer– a stubby over-and-under .41-caliber Remington. The kind old-time gamblers toted. Small, but powerful enough to do significant damage.

"Mighty strange hours for a dentist," Jonah said.

Whitehall smiled. "And for meddling constables as well." He aimed the stubby barrel directly at Jonah's face. "Away from the chair, please."

Jonah did as he requested. Soon, the two had slowly exchanged places. The sheriff stood by the doorway, while the dentist stood beside the adjustable chair. The old man took the dental file, stepped backward, and opened the door of a supply closet. Without turning on the inside light, he laid the file on a shelf somewhere inside and closed the door behind him.

"So," said Jonah. "Let's have that little chat."

"Yes, let us do that." The dentist stared down at the gun in his hand. "You know, I so despise these things. No subtly to one at all... no grace. Just pull the trigger and bang. Firearms aren't as common where I come from as they are here. They usually belong to retired military officers or those imbeciles at Scotland Yard."

Jonah's eyes were on the little pistol. Whitehall's hand was relaxed and steady. "Ah, yes... your old nemesis."

The elderly man smiled softly. "Now, I really couldn't consider them as such. They never came within twenty city blocks of me. Whitechapel is where they focused their attention... not in the prosperous, upscale part of town where I resided."

"Those women... back in London... why did you do it?"

Whitehall laughed. It was disturbing sound. "Why does it perplex you law officers so? The reasons why? I live in mazes of the mind, Constable. Mazes so dark and convoluted that you would be hopelessly lost in them and never find your way out." The dentist looked distastefully at the gun in his hand. He returned it to his pocket, while the opposite hand withdrew a knife from the other. It was long and wickedly curved. The handle was of polished mother-of-pearl.

"Is that your weapon of choice?" Jonah asked him.

That grin again– thin, skeletal, unsettling. "I prefer to regard it as a tool."

"What are you going to do with it? Cut my head off?"

Whitehall considered that to be greatly amusing. "Oh, no, Constable! I would never subject you to such a trite and disrespectful act. You have gained my respect. For you there would be special things. Prolonged things." The old man's smile broadened. "You have no comprehension of the amount of damage the human body can endure before death finally claims it."

For a long moment, silence. The air between them seemed as thick as blood.

"I could draw this gun and shoot you right now," the sheriff told him.

"Yes," Nigel Whitehall said. There was a hot, feverish cast to the dentist's eyes. His lean body seemed taut, like the spring of a clock wound one turn too tightly. "You could certainly try."

Jonah looked at the hand that held the knife. The knuckles were as white as bone. Two long-legged steps, maybe three, and the blade would be inside him. The sheriff's own sidearm, heavy against his hip, seemed deceptively distant from his right hand.

"Please." Whitehall's voice was soft, almost trembling as it pleaded. "Try."

Jonah had fought Germans in the Argonne Forest. He had been a law officer for nearly ten years and had faced abusive husbands and cutthroat moonshiners. He was fair-minded, but tough as nails. He backed down to no man. But this was no ordinary man… if he could even be considered a man at all.

He eased his hand away from his holster and backed away.

Whitehall seemed disappointed. "Constable… you are not nearly as obtuse as I thought."

"You won't get another one," Jonah warned him. "You'll not make another jack-o'-lantern."

The elderly gentleman just grinned. Brought the knife up and fingered the blade with his other hand. Ran the edge against the ball of his thumb and drew blood. Never flinched a muscle.

"I'll be watching." The sheriff eased backward toward the doorway of the waiting room. "I don't have the evidence to convict you just yet… but, sooner or later, I will."

The blade bit deeply. Past muscle… scraping bone.

And, still, he smiled.

"Good evening, Constable. And Happy Halloween."

A moment later, Jonas was outside. He shut the door and leaned with his back against it, breathing in the cool, October air.

He walked along the sidewalk and made his way down the street to his car. Whitehall had already done his work for that night. Tomorrow night was Halloween.

Despite the sheriff's warning, Whitehall would make his move then.

After all, what was All Hallows' Eve without its jack-o'-lantern?

The following evening, around five o'clock, Jonah called his wife from the office.

"Sorry I didn't make it to supper, but that son of a bitch is going to make his move again tonight and I've got to be ready," he explained.

"I understand," Millicent said. "So… you really know who it is."

"Yes." Jonah didn't give her time to say more on the subject.

"Are you about to take the young'uns trick-or-treating?"

"We're about to leave now," she said. "You ought to see their costumes. They're so cute."

A stretch of tense silence hung between them.

"Sweetheart... you remember that old gun I brought back from the War? The Colt .45 slide-action... the one I taught you to shoot?"

"I remember."

"Do me a favor," he said, not giving her a chance to protest. "Get it out of my nightstand drawer and put it in your purse. Just to be on the safe side."

"All right." Another moment of silence. "Jonah... honey, be careful."

"I will. I love you."

"Love you, too. To the moon and back."

Jonah hung up the phone and stood there with a sick sensation in the pit of his stomach. He went to the gun case across the room and took a Winchester Model 12 pump shotgun from its cradle. He emptied a box of shells into his jacket pocket, then checked the rounds in his revolver and returned it to its holster.

A few minutes later, Jonah was parked across the street in front of Nigel Whitehall's house on Willowbrook Avenue. Twilight had already fallen and it was dark out. The porch light of the dentist's home was on and the windows were lit up. He watched as the old man moved from room to room, his shadow showing against the drawn blinds.

One hour passed into another. Still, Whitehall stayed put and failed to leave the house. Trick-or-treaters came and went, making their rounds, filling their pillowcases and paper sacks with treats. Around seven-thirty, Millicent showed up with Matthew and Vickie. They waved at Jonah, but didn't approach his car, knowing that he was on duty.

There was a tense moment when Whitehall opened the door to the children's calls of "Trick-or-treat!" Jonah could imagine the old man grabbing his babies, pulling them inside, and locking the door behind him. But, of course, he didn't. He simply deposited a bright red apple in each one's bag... and looked directly across the street, straight at Jonah, with a big smile on his gaunt face.

After a while, all the trick-or-treaters had finished for the night. The street in front of the Whitehall house grew empty and quiet. Still, the windows of the little house remained lit. Every now and then, the tall, old man could be seen inside, moving around.

Nine o'clock passed, leading into ten, then eleven. Despite the urgency of his surveillance, Jonah felt himself growing tired and restless. Several times he nodded off, only to awake with a jolt. He would look toward the house and see that nothing had changed. The windows were still bright with lamplight and Whitehall's old black Ford Model T was still parked in the driveway, where it had been all evening.

Eventually, the sheriff's weariness got the best of him. He fell asleep and snoozed for an indeterminate period of time. He awoke when he dreamt that someone reached through the open window of the Packard and laid the cold steel of a knife blade against his throat. Jonah sat up in his seat with a start, finding no one there.

But had there been?

He looked down and found something lying in the lap of his britches. It was a pale square of beige cardboard. A library card.

Speckled with blood.

"Oh shit!" He looked toward the house. The lights were off and the Ford was nowhere to be seen.

Jonah started his engine and made a U-turn in the narrow street, heading for town. When he reached the library, he jumped out, taking the shotgun with him. He worked the pump and jacked a shell into the chamber, then ran up the walkway.

The front door was unlocked and open. Cautiously, he stepped inside. The building was pitch dark... except for a faint glow beyond the bookshelves. He walked slowly through the gloom, until he emerged into the main chamber of the library.

"Oh, God," he muttered, when he saw the source of the muted light. "No."

The head of Gladys Willoughby sat in the center of the librarian's desk. Flickering light emanated from the empty holes of her eye sockets, the double slits of her severed nose, and the slack, gaping mouth of erratic teeth. She looked both shocked and disappointed... as though realizing that she wasn't quite as smart as she originally thought.

Jonah looked beyond the jack-o'-lantern and saw the headless body of Miss Gladys sitting in her librarian chair, dressed in a flower-print nightgown. A note had been pinned to her chest. It read *Shhhh! Quiet Please!*

It was the object that did the pinning that disturbed the sheriff. Holding the paper in place, impaling the shallow chest of the old woman, was the dental file that Whitehall had used to smooth the sharp edges of Matthew's broken tooth.

He's been to his office!

Jonah turned and ran for the door. He left his car parked where it was and, a moment later, approached the open door of the dentist office. The lights were on... bright, but far from inviting.

He entered the front door, directing the barrel of the 12-gauge ahead of him. When he reached the examination room, he found it empty. The old man wasn't there. The steel tray was bare on the rolling table. All the instruments were gone.

Jonah Townshend turned his eyes to the storage closet. There was a note pinned to the wooden panel with a curved dental pick.

Slowly, he approached the door and stared at the note that had been left for him. It read:

Back to Hell...

My Dearest Constable,

Survival has always been my most precious commodity. Every now and then, I encounter someone such as you... someone with the tenacity and determination to rob me of my carnal pleasures and, ultimately, my liberty. And, so, it has brought about this night... this exceedingly busy Halloween night. You were clever, Constable Townshend. Very clever... as was the librarian. Unfortunately, for her, not quite clever—or cautious—enough.

And, so, I shall bid you farewell. I have left my parting regards to those who matter most and sojourn onward. Perhaps I shall seek warmer climates. Texas or New Mexico. Maybe Arizona. Someplace where the local constable has never heard of the Wraith of Whitechapel, or even cares.

Feast well upon your regret, Jonah.

It is a meal best served hot, like the flow of fresh blood from the vein. Like the hot tears of sorrow, bitter and contrite.

Most Respectfully Yours,
Nigel Whitehall
J.T.R.

Jonah stood there and stared at the letter for a long moment. Then he noticed that the door of the supply closet was slightly open and that a light shone from inside.

Don't go in, warned his thoughts, *you don't want to see what's there.*

But he went anyway.

Once inside, he looked directly ahead. Against the far wall there was shelving. On those shelves were a dozen or so Mason jars. Each had a piece of white surgical tape plastered to the glass. And on each tape was written a name.

Mary Ann. Annie. Elizabeth. Catherine. Mary Jane.

Other jars bore additional names... of both women and men.

Inside the containers floated things in milky yellow formaldehyde. Jonah was no physician, but he could imagine what they were. Kidneys, bladders, spleens... a woman's ovaries... the twin testes of a man.

Then there were three more jars. Empty... the tops unscrewed and laid aside.

The names on these vessels were horribly and grievously familiar.

"*No!*" screamed Jonah Townshend.

Without hesitation, he turned and ran.

He pulled into the crushed gravel drive of his property five minutes later. The front of the house looked normal for that time of night. The windows were dark, but the children's jack-o'-lanterns were lit, casting flickering light across the leaf-strewn yard.

The Packard had scarcely come to a halt before he was out of the vehicle and running around the rear of the house, his revolver drawn and cocked. He bounded up the back-porch steps and yanked open the screen door with a squeal of unoiled hinges. The kitchen just beyond was pitch black.

He smelled an aroma he hadn't encountered for many years.

The coppery stench of profaned flesh and fresh blood.

The reek of violent and profuse death.

"Millicent?" he asked. His voice was hoarse and utterly devoid of hope.

He reached out, found the light switch, and turned it on.

His wife was on the kitchen table.

And on the counters... the stove... the icebox.

Dangling from the light fixture. Spread across the kitchen floor.

He recalled the photograph of Mary Kelly. This... this was a dozen... a thousand... times worse.

Jonah took a couple of stumbling steps into the room. His left foot hit something plump and moist. It burst beneath the sole of his boot. A liver? A breast, bloodless and blind? The motionless sack of Millie's liberated heart... the arteries and ventricles severed by a surgeon's masterful cut?

The sheriff staggered from the room and into the adjoining hallway just beyond. He dropped heavily to his knees and vomited violently. When dry heaves were all that remained and his head began to clear, he leapt to his feet and ran for the staircase, his heart pounding.

"Matthew!" he shrieked. "Vickie!" His feet pounded the risers as he climbed to the upper floor. Jonah ran down the corridor, past his and Millie's bedroom, toward the two bedrooms at the far end.

He checked Vickie's room first. The sheets of the bed were tangled. Her teddy bear, Mister Snuggles, lay abandoned on the floor. Face to the floor, as though hiding his button eyes from what had taken place.

Moonlight shown through the bedroom window, casting a

pale glow upon Vickie's pillow. Tiny spots dotted the material...
ink black in darkness... but much more vibrant come broad
daylight.

An instant later, Jonah was across the hall, in Matthew's
room. The boy had put up a fight. His bedclothes were strewn
across the floor, also dark and splattered.

Something rested atop his son's pillow. A White Owl cigar
box.

Dr. Whitehall's prize box.

With a trembling hand, Jonah lifted the lid and looked
inside.

Gifts awaited him. Prizes that his mind would, unfortunately, possess forever.

A pair of dental pliers, glistening and wet.

Tiny bits of ivory, some bigger than others. One chipped,
but smooth to the touch.

And a note for his eyes only... written in a bold, but elegant
hand.

The words on the slip of paper were cryptic, but horrible.
The poetry of a lunatic.

Stunned, he left the room and walked to the stairs. Jonah
descended the staircase, crossed the foyer, and went outside. He
left the front porch and stumbled down the steps, unable to feel
his feet beneath him. He felt cold, numb... dead, yet somehow
still alive.

He stopped in the center of the sidewalk and called out his
children's names. But there was no resonance to it. They came
out as bitter and unalterable as names chiseled into granite
above wilted flowers.

With a moan—an awful, hollow sound that lacked substance
or sanity—he turned and looked back at the porch.

There were four jack-o'-lanterns on the porch railing.

Matthew and Vickie had only carved two of them.

The other two, small and round, smiled at him. Eyes brilliant. Picket-fence grins.

One wore a witch's hat. The other that of a cowboy.

Jonah's fingers grew slack and loosened. The note... the final
farewell... dropped from his grasp and settled to the stones of

the walkway amid the husks of shriveled autumn leaves.

The words no longer held mystery. They were as clear as clear could be.

See the porch, all aglow,
Pretty little lanterns all in a row.

THE AMAZING
AND TOTALLY AWESOME
FRIGHT CREATURE!

"What are you? A doofus or something? You can't order things like that anymore... and certainly not for a dollar fifty!"

Aaron looked up from the yellowed copy of *The Invincible Iron Man* #162, annoyed by Rickey's comment. But then, his best friend was one big, overweight bundle of irritation and exasperation, with precious little tact and restraint to keep it all from spilling out. Rickey pretty much said what he thought, 24/7, and most of it had to do with how lame or stupid Aaron's ideas or interests were. Sometimes it really got on his last nerve, but they had been buddies since preschool and it was hard to chuck a relationship that tight, even if the guy was a genuine pain in the ass.

It was a rainy afternoon in mid-September when they dug through Aaron's dad's old comic book collection in the storage closet of the garage. Rickey was gorging on snacks and flipping through copies of *Batman* and *The Flash*, only interested in the pictures and not the storylines. Aaron had gone from *Justice League of America* to *The Fantastic Four*, and was midway through *The Invincible Iron Man*, when the advertisement in the back of the comic drew his attention. It was surrounded by other vintage mail order ads: ENTERTAINING AND INCREDIBLE LIVE SEA MONKEYS!, COUNT DANTE... THE DEADLIEST MAN ALIVE! JOIN THE BLACK DRAGON FIGHTING SOCIETY!...

PATENTED 3-D HYPNO-COIN... FREE, WITH 25 LESSONS IN HYPNOTISM! and MAKE MONEY...GET PRIZES... WITH FAST-SELLING AMERICAN SEEDS!

The one that caught his eye was different. It showed a long, lion-maned, spike-backed monstrosity with wildly evil eyes, a mouthful of fangs, and claws that could really do some major damage to the human anatomy. The text underneath read: AMAZING AND TOTALLY AWESOME FRIGHT CREATURE! NOT A TOY... A REAL, LIVING, BREATHING MONSTER TO OWN AND RAISE! WATCH IT GROW BEFORE YOUR VERY EYES! AMAZE AND IMPRESS YOUR FRIENDS AS IT OBEYS YOUR EVERY COMMAND! ORDER YOURS TODAY FOR ONLY $1.50 (plus 25 cents shipping and handling) HURRY... BEFORE IT BECOMES EXTINCT!

Rickey leaned over and peeked over his shoulder, snorting through his nose.

"God! Just look at it! They just took an old drawing of a Chinese dragon and doctored it up. Probably something rubber. Everything that cheap from comic books was made of rubber back then."

"It claims that it's alive," Aaron replied. "Wouldn't it be cool to have something like that... maybe to feed and raise and take out with you on Halloween night when you go trick-or-treating?" All Hallows' Eve happened to be Aaron's favorite holiday, even more than Christmas. "Maybe it could help us fend off the Baxter Brothers when they try to extort us for candy this year."

"Well, even if it was alive—which it wasn't—you can't order it anymore. That issue came out in, what... 1982? That company probably isn't even in business anymore after thirty-five years!"

"Thirty-eight years," Aaron corrected him, doing the math in his head.

Rickey shook his head in disgust and looked around. "Hey, has your old man got any *Mad* or *Cracked*? Or maybe *Vampirella*." He licked his lips—which were orange with Cheetos dust. "Yeah that spooky brunette babe with her boobs spilling out of the front of her costume!"

Aaron ignored his pal's display of pre-teen lust and looked back at the ad. Yeah, thirty-eight years was a long time. But it would have been great to have raised and trained your very own personal Amazing and Totally Awesome Fright Creature.

That night, after his parents had gone to bed, Aaron powered up his Chromebook and, out of sheer curiosity, Googled "Amazing and Totally Awesome Fright Creature". He figured an image of the advertisement would pop up or maybe someone's blog about old vintage comic book ads. Instead, he was surprised when an entry for J&S Unique Imports surfaced. He instantly clicked on the link and found himself looking at a much more gruesome and scary rendering of the Fright Creature. The description was pretty much the same as it had been in the comic book, but the price was a tad higher—$20 plus $5.99 shipping.

He checked the name of the company again. The Iron Man comic had it as Jock and Smitty's Novelties & Curiosities, Inc. Could this be the same mail order outfit, still in business after all these years?

He stared into that grisly, fang-filled face with the ivory spikes on its back and the wicked, curved claws. And he just had to have it.

Aaron reached over and grabbed his cell phone. His parents had gotten it for his last birthday, in case he needed to call from school or because of an emergency. He brought up his contacts and punched an icon of a big, pink pig at an eating trough. It rang a couple of times before Rickey picked up. "Hmmm? Yeah?" He could tell from his pillow-muffled voice that his friend had been sound asleep.

"Do you still have that PayPal account for getting paid for mowing yards?"

"Who the shit is this?"

"You know who," Aaron snapped. "Well, do you?"

"Sure," Rickey said with a yawn. "My dad set it up for me. Why?"

"How much do you have in there?"

"I don't know. Maybe thirty… thirty-two dollars."

Aaron grinned broadly. "You wanna go halfsies on a cool Amazing and Totally Awesome Fright Creature?"

"What? Are you still obsessing over that idiotic comic book

ad? I told you, that company..."

"... is still in business," Aaron blurted. "And they still have it in stock!"

Rickey was suddenly silent. Jeff could hear the faint squeak of mattress springs as his pal sat up in bed. "Really?"

"Really!"

"How much?"

"Only twenty dollars plus five ninety-nine shipping and handling."

"Gee, that's kind of expensive, isn't it? Couldn't we find it cheaper somewhere else?"

It was Aaron's turn to snort through his nose, an annoying gesture that he found utterly satisfying and justified at that very moment. "DUH! You can't just run down to the Dollar General Store and buy a genuine Fright Creature, do you think?"

"No... I reckon not." Rickey could really dish out the sarcasm, but he had a hard time swallowing it. "Well... how much do you have? I'm not paying for the whole thing."

"I've got five bucks my grandmother gave me for cleaning out her fence row last month and eight more for babysitting... uh... the kids next door." Aaron groaned inwardly. The awful secret had just spilled out, without him even thinking.

Rickey not only laughed, he literally guffawed. "Babysitting? Oh, my, Miss Aaron Mae, could you please look after the little ones while I run to the grocery store? Could you wipe their snotty noses and change their doody diapers? And, of course, my dear, you can have a tea party with little Suzy and Tommy. You can bake cookies in your Easy Bake Oven and, afterwards, you can all play with Barbies and American Girl dolls!'

Aaron said nothing, just sat there with his ears blazing like Ghost Rider's skull, until Rickey's laughter gradually died down. "Are you done?" he finally asked.

His rotund friend let out another chuckle or two before answering. "Yeah... yeah, I'm finished. Thanks for that. It was priceless."

"Well... are we going to do it?"

Rickey seemed to think for a moment. "Oh... all right! If you put in thirteen dollars, I'll pay the rest. The money's linked

to my dad's Master Card. I'll sneak it out of his wallet and we'll
order it online tomorrow after school."

"Freaking fantastic!" Aaron wanted to say the "other"
F-word, but his mom had ears like a German shepherd and
could detect profanity before you could get it halfway out of
your mouth, even if she was in a coma.

After he set his phone back on the nightstand, he laid there,
basking in the glow of the Chromebook screen, staring into the
crazy, blood-shot eyes of the thing that would soon regard him
as "master"... or, at least, "half-master" considering that Rickey
owned an equal share.

After that, they checked Rickey's mailbox regularly.

They figured that they would either find a slip that said a
package was waiting for them at the post office or find a big
box from UPS on the door mat of Rickey's porch. After all, an
Amazing and Totally Awesome Fright Creature just had to
arrive in a sizable container.

It was on a Wednesday in the second week of October that
they checked the mailbox and found a small box sitting on top
of a stack of bills.

Aaron picked it up and appraised it with disappointment.
It was barely the size of a pack of cigarettes... and not the king-
sized ones either.

Rickey scowled. "Naw."

"Yeah." Aaron looked at the label. "It's from J&S Imports."

His buddy's broad face reddened. "I knew it! What a load of
bullshit!" He grabbed the box and shook it violently. Something
inside rattled.

Aaron reached over and grabbed it. "Stop that! You'll kill
it!"

"There's nothing alive inside. There are no air holes... see? I
bet it's a rubber centipede or roach."

"Well, let's go in your garage and take a look," Aaron suggested. Even as his spirits sank to rock bottom, he still hoped
that something good might come out of this mail order screw-
ing they had received.

A few minutes later, the two boys knelt on the oil-stained

floor of Rickey's garage. Carefully, Aaron opened the end of the box and dumped its contents onto the concrete.

A small creature that resembled a blue lizard skittered out of the cramped confinement of the little carton. It looked sleepy and disoriented at first, then shook its tiny head and blinked at them with bug eyes the size of M&Ms... the plain kind, not the peanut.

"A salamander," mumbled Rickey, stunned. "They took our twenty-five ninety-nine and sent us a freaking salamander."

"It doesn't look like a salamander to me," Aaron told him. He poked at the thing with the tip of his finger. It opened its tiny mouth and licked at it with a slimy green tongue. "It must be a baby Scare Creature."

"Well, I say we take a loss on our investment and flush it down the toilet."

Aaron was horrified. "Hell no, you won't!" He picked up the little creature in his hand and was surprised at how cold and clammy it was. "We're going to feed and raise it, just like we planned."

Rickey laughed. "If you think it's going to sprout fangs, spikes, and claws and look like that thing in the advertisement, it's you we ought to flush like a brainless turd. What are we supposed to feed it anyway?"

Aaron fished a slip of paper from the little box and unfolded it. "It says here that he likes meat. Hamburger, chicken, bacon... stuff like that."

"I might spring for a cheap pack of wieners from Aldi or something. Or we could just dig some earthworms out of the back yard and save us a dollar-fifty."

He stared at Rickey like he was an idiot. "This is a unique organism. Maybe even an urban legend. It's an Amazing and Totally Awesome Fright Creature! Do you think worms are going to satisfy its monstrous cravings? Do you think it's going to obey our every command if we feed it garbage?"

"I reckon not," admitted Rickey. "What are we going to do with it? Where are we going to put it?"

"Remember when you had that pet iguana? Do you still have that aquarium with the screened lid and the light bulb?"

"Yeah, it's around here somewhere," said the boy. "Who's gonna keep it? My mom had enough of the iguana... said I could never have another pet in the house, especially when she woke up in the middle of the night with that lizard tangled up in her hair. You should've heard her scream!"

"I can keep it in my room," Aaron suggested. "My parents never come in my room. All my horror stuff creeps them out, so they just leave me alone."

"Okay," agreed Rickey, "but I get to visit it whenever I want."

"Sure. It's half yours. We'll raise it together... watch it turn into that hideous fiend that's in the comic book ad."

Rickey laughed. "That thing? Don't get your hopes up. And that idea you had about taking it trick-or-treating with us... it'll never happen. It's only a couple of weeks till Halloween. It'll probably get sick and die by then."

"Just find the aquarium, will you?" Aaron said.

As his pal began to rummage through the junk in the garage, the boy in the eyeglasses stroked the tiny creature in the palm of his hand. Its back arched and it made a tiny sound like a cat purring. *I'll take good care of you*, Aaron promised silently. *I believe in you, even if Rickey doesn't. You'll make it to Halloween, I swear. Then we'll show them. Everyone will see just how amazing and totally awesome you really are."*

They named it Fang. It was sort of an odd choice, considering the thing practically had no teeth in its head. But, as it turned out, it wasn't very long until the little critter lived up to his name.

Fang began to grow steadily in the days leading up to Halloween. It started out the size of a mouse, then a hamster, then a full-grown guinea pig. Its skin took on a weird, translucent appearance that seemed to change colors—green, purple, blue, red, orange—depending on what angle it was turned at the moment. Tiny nubs in its wide jaws sharpened to points and began to lengthen into wickedly sharp fangs. Fuzz formed around his neck, thickening, growing dark and stringy, and small spikes sprouted down the length of its backbone.

By the time Fang had reached the size of a black lab puppy, its teeth were two inches long and could slice a sheet of wide-rule notebook paper clean in half. Its feet grew from chubby paws to long-toed feet that sort of resembled a monkey's nimble hands... except for the hooked claws at the tips of each digit. And the claws were twice as sharp as the spikes on Fang's back. Aaron and Rickey had taken to putting on leather work gloves from Rickey's dad's toolbox to avoid all the nicks and cuts they were getting from handling the creature. Before long, they didn't want to pick it up at all, if they could avoid it.

By the Thursday before Halloween, Fang began to actually resemble that illustration in the comic book advertisement. It was both satisfying (they didn't feel cheated) and disturbing (just what the hell had they gotten themselves into?)

By Saturday morning, they decided to move Fang out of Aaron's bedroom to the garage. The ten-gallon aquarium, which was becoming more and more inadequate, sat across the room from Aaron's bed, and Fang paced back and forth all night long, its clawed feet scratching and scrabbling on the rocky floor of the bottom of the container. Also, it began to emit a low, unnerving growl in the dead of night, especially when it was hungry... which seemed to be a constant thing now. Ball Park Franks and Chicken McNuggets had seemed to satisfy its hunger at first, but soon it demanded more and more meat. The boys began pooling their allowances to buy raw hamburger from the grocery store and Rickey had even sneaked a couple of ribeye steaks from his mom's freezer. Keeping their mail-order pet fed and satisfied was beginning to prove to be both expensive and risky.

Then on Sunday afternoon after lunch, they went to check on Fang and it was gone. The screen mesh of the lid had been ripped open and peeled back. "Oh crap!" moaned Rickey. "Where'd he go to?"

"He's gotta be around here somewhere," Aaron said, trying to keep his cool. They searched the garage from top to bottom... but no Fang was to be found.

The two were leaving the garage to search the neighborhood, when they heard noises from the bushes near the swing set. They were nasty-sounding noises... the rip and tear of something moist and the hollow splinter and crack of something being chewed and broken.

Cautiously, they walked over and peeked into the shadows between two shrubs. What they saw nearly made them puke.

"Aw, shit, man..." said Rickey with a groan. "What is that thing?"

Aaron adjusted his glasses and swallowed a little bile that had come up in his throat. "I think it's Mrs. Hanover's cat. Mister Boots."

Or what was *left* of Mister Boots. Fang had torn the feline open from throat to cat nuts and was feasting on what was inside. Sharp claws shredded flesh and muscle, while wicked fangs tore and devoured internal organs. The forked, green tongue—which was unnervingly long and serpentine now—lapped up blood and brains, hungrily and greedily.

"Uh, Fang." Aaron's voice was a nervous croak as he spoke. "Whatcha doing, boy?"

Fang lifted its head, roughly the size of a Nerf football now, and stared at them. It was at that moment that the thing's eyes struck them for the first time. The illustration in the comic book ad seemed to be complete now. Fang's eyes were wide, bloodshot, and crazy. Downright insane.

Aaron remembered seeing an old copy of *Life* magazine at a yard sale once, one that had the Manson family on the front cover. *Oh my God! He has Charlie's crazy-ass eyes!*

"What are we gonna do?" asked Rickey. "Go tell Mrs. Hanover?"

"Are you nuts? She'll fall over dead with a stroke. Let's just take poor Mister Boots and bury him. If anyone finds out what Fang's done, they'll take him away from us."

"Yeah," agreed Rickey. "They'll haul him off to the monster pound and give him the sleep shot."

Slowly, Aaron took a few steps forward. "Uh... Fang."

The creature lifted its head from the depths of Mister Boot's belly, its teeth gripping a twisted length of intestine. Fang growled low in its throat and its back arched slightly, the spikes looking like small bull horns along its spine, ready to gore and impale.

"Why don't we just let him finish and then we'll do the bury-ing?" suggested Rickey.

Aaron agreed with a nod and slowly backed away.

After the Amazing and Totally Awesome Scare Creature had devoured every bit of muscle, flesh, and hide, and sucked every bit of pink marrow from the cat's shattered bones, its frenzied eyes grew heavy and it curled into a ball and fell gently to sleep. While Aaron picked up what was left of poor Mister Boots and deposited it in a Walmart sack for burial, Rickey carefully lifted the sleeping creature using the Wells Lamont gloves. "Damn!" he whispered. "Ol' Fang is getting heavy. I'd say he's close to twelve pounds now. Maybe more."

They took it back to its aquarium lair without waking it. Aaron found an old metal serving tray and placed it on top, then weighted it down with a greasy car battery they found under the tool bench.

"Do you think it'll hold it?" asked Rickey.

"I sure hope so," Aaron told him. *But for how long?*

Together, they took the soggy Walmart bag and a shovel and, without drawing attention, went to a shady spot beneath a maple tree and laid the remnants of Fang's lunch to rest.

By the time Halloween night rolled around, Fang was nearly the size of a border collie. They had abandoned the cramped aquar-ium and placed it in a medium-sized kennel cage that Rickey found at the local dump. They had hidden him away in some underbrush in Aaron's back yard so their parents wouldn't know. Raising Fang had been sort of fun and interesting at first. Now it was just stressful and more than a little frightening.

Aaron had chosen to go dressed as Harry Potter and Rickey went as Hagrid. They took Fang with them, secured by a dog collar and leash. The scare creature seemed excited to be out and about, but they were surprised when it behaved itself and didn't try to attack anyone. After what happened to Mister Boots, they were afraid it would go berserk in a crowd of trick-or-treaters, especially if one were dressed like Catwoman or Hello Kitty or something.

The reaction they received at the sight of their Amazing

and Totally Awesome Fright Creature wasn't exactly what they expected. At first, they got wide-eyed stares, then the kids around them—even the little ones—started giggling and laughing.

"Doesn't look like our scare creature is scary enough, does it?" said Rickey, rolling his eyes. "This thing was supposed to make us cool. We were supposed to be feared and respected, not laughed off the face of the earth."

Aaron tried to ignore his pal, but he was right. This certainly wasn't working out the way the advertisement promised.

They trick-or-treated for an hour, going from house to house in their neighborhood. When they came to Mrs. Hanover's house, the elderly woman smiled and placed handfuls of Sixlets and Smarties into their bags. She regarded Fang and, like everyone else, began to laugh. "I love your dog's costume!"

"But, it's not a costu—" Rickey began, then was jarred into silence by his best friend's elbow.

"Thanks, Mrs. Hanover," Aaron said politely.

Before she shut her front door, her face grew sort of sad. "By the way, boys, you haven't seen Mister Boots around, have you?"

"No, ma'am. But we'll sure let you know if we do."

As they were heading back down the walkway to the street, Fang unleashed a noxious fart that stank like roadkill on a hot August day.

"Why, there's Mister Boots right there," said Rickey with a bearded grin.

"Shut up, before someone hears you!" snapped Aaron. "Let's go over to Willclay Avenue and try our luck there. I hear they give out some good stuff."

They cut down an alleyway, intending to take a shortcut. They hadn't gotten halfway when two forms stood up from behind a couple of trash cans. Aaron and Rickey stopped dead in their tracks, their hearts pounding. They knew exactly who it was.

It was the notorious Baxter Brothers—twins who looked completely the opposite of one another. The thin, short one—Brent—was decked out as Freddy Krueger, while Billy, the big tall one, was dressed like Leatherface from *The Texas Chain Saw Massacre*. Their father was the butcher at the Kroger store on Main Street and Billy wore his long, white work apron, splattered with genuine animal blood.

"Hey!" said Brent, beckoning with his razored glove. "Get your asses over here!'

"Yeah," said Billy. "We've been looking all over for you. It's time to pay up. We need candy."

"Come on, guys," said Rickey. "Not this year, okay?"

"No. Not okay. Hand it over now."

Aaron simply smiled. "Fang... *attack!*"

But Fang didn't attack. Instead, he retreated and stood behind his two helpless masters.

"I think your dog is ready to piss itself," Billy said with a chuckle. "And I bet you are, too. Now give us the candy or we'll make you stick your peckers in the knothole of that fence over there. I swear we will."

Brent doubled over and laughed loudly. "You'll be pulling splinters out of your junk for days!"

Aaron didn't turn around, but pulled at the leash sharply. "Come on, Fang, dammit! You're embarrassing me."

"What kinda dog is that anyway?" asked Billy. "A shit-zoo?"

As his twin brother cackled at his lame joke, Aaron gave the leash another sharp tug. Surprisingly, the length of leather and the broken collar it was attached to came flying up to lie at his feet. "That the...?"

Strange noises were coming from behind Aaron and Rickey. The crackling of disjointed bones and muscles stretching and reforming. Instead of the cool chill of the October night, the pair felt a hot, fetid heat scorch the napes of their necks.

Rickey glanced over his shoulder and his eyes bugged, big and bright, in the gloom of the alleyway. "Oh... shit."

Before Aaron could turn around, something huge leapt over them and landed in the gravel between them and the Baxter Brothers.

It was Fang... but it wasn't the Fang of a few seconds ago. The thing had grown to five times its former size. The spikes on its back were curved and wickedly sharp, like the horns of a bull, and its teeth were as long as his mom's knitting needles. The claws at the end of its nimble fingers were hooked and looked sharp enough to decapitate with one fatal swipe. Fang had transformed into something that was ten times more terrifying than the illustration in the comic book advertisement. It was amazing. It was totally awesome. And it was certainly scary as hell!

The Baxter Brother only stood there at first. Then they screamed and turned to run, but didn't get far. Fang's green tongue lashed out and wrapped around Brent Baxter's skinny neck. The scare creature's abdomen opened, revealing a dark cavity that stank of decay and sulfur. With a yank, Fang tossed Brent into the pouch, then grabbed his brother by his ankles, held him dangling in mid-air for a long moment, then deposited him in the hole as well.

Aaron and Rickey heard the brothers' screams of absolute terror, then heard them no more as the slit in Fang's belly closed tightly shut. The creature winked at them with one huge, crazy eye and grinned with a mouthful of fangs that would make Jaws look like a petty little goldfish.

The two boys dropped their trick-or-treat bags and began to run in the opposite direction. At the same time, Fang whirled and disappeared into the darkness of night.

"I think we made a *big* mistake," Rickey said as they headed for home.

Aaron agreed. "Yeah... we should have gone with the Sea Monkeys."

On the edge of a dark forest, hunkered amid leafy kudzu and a carpet of dry, autumn leaves, waited two forms. They were cloaked in shadow... completely indistinguishable at first. Then the clouds parted and a full moon shown through the crooked tree limbs above. Pale light glistened on glossy scales and bristly fur, then slowly swept across the face of the road sign they crouched beside. It was rectangular, peppered with .22 bullet holes and rust, and read WELCOME TO FEAR COUNTY.

"Where the hell is he?" one of them grumbled. Its jagged

fangs rubbed, one against the other, grating in aggravation.

"Don't worry," hissed the other one. "He'll be here."

"If he doesn't get his spiny ass in gear, we'll miss the celebration. The Elder Fiend will be royally pissed if he doesn't get his quota of sacrifices tonight."

"You're just one big bundle of sunshine and rainbows tonight, aren't you?"

"That was a low blow, Critter. Maybe my attitude wouldn't stink if he would just be on time for once. I'm punctual, so why not him?" The beast, who resembled an oversized rat, cocked its narrow head. "You don't think he got caught, do you?"

"Relax, Thing. He didn't get caught. He's smarter than that. He is amazing and totally awesome, you know."

"Amazing my ass! That's just how he hypes himself up to get in. You know, we thought Sasquatch was smart, too, until he was strolling through the woods without a care in the world and that guy caught him on film. If the footage hadn't been so unfocused and grainy, he might have ended up in a damn zoo or his big-ass feet hanging on some hunter's wall."

They heard the snap of a fallen tree branch and the sound of heavy footfalls in the underbrush. "Creature? Is that you?" asked Critter.

Suddenly, the third of the trio stepped into sight, looking weary and irritated. "Yeah, yeah... it's me. Sorry I was late. Things got kinda crazy at the end."

Critter chuckled. "Don't they always? Did you have trouble getting in?"

Creature shook his horned head in disgust. "Do you know how slow the postal service is these days? 'Snail-mail' doesn't do it justice. It's like watching paint dry. If that novelty company had mailed me Priority or FedEx, I'd have been on top of my game."

"Quit your bellyaching!" snapped Thing, his silvery eyes narrowing. "At least you don't have to lay by the side of the road and play dead until someone comes by and pokes you with a freaking stick."

"We all have our burdens to bear," Critter said

diplomatically. "A monster's path is rife with obstacles and misfortune. Do you have your contributions?"

"I've got a couple of live ones stashed away in my pouch," Creature admitted. "I'll be glad to get 'em out of there, too. It feels like they're sucker-punching my kidneys."

"How about you, Thing?"

The monster looked down at a large sack made of hide and black and gray-striped fur. "I only got one... but it's a big one." Inside, they could hear someone gibbering madly and laughing from time to time.

The other two looked at him skeptically. "You didn't mess this one up, did you?"

Thing grinned sheepishly. "Well... I sort of bit his foot off and ripped his back open." The other two looked at one another. Thing was known to have an insatiable spine fetish. "Oh... and I did eat his wife. And chomped off a deputy's head. But that's all."

"That's just great!" said Creature in exasperation. "You know how the Elder Fiend frowns on damaged goods."

"Let's just get going," suggested Critter. He picked up two children cocooned in snakeskin and slung them over his serpentine shoulders. "We're running late already."

As they prepared to leave, Creature looked over at Critter. "So, who is the Master of Ceremonies this year? Cthulhu? Kraken? The Mothman?"

"Uh... no. None of them were available so they got Quetzalcoatl."

Thing rolled his silver eyes. "That blowhard of a flying snake with the wings and feathers? He's so puffed-up and longwinded! We'll be lucky to get to the buffet by midnight."

Critter hissed and gritted his fangs so hard that venom trickled down his chin. "Hey, show a little respect, will you? You're talking about family here! Q is my third cousin on my mother's side. He's a freaking god, for Hell's sake! And he can fly. You can't do that, can you, Thing?"

The mutant rat shook his narrow head. "No... I can't fly worth a lick. But I can open and close a car door with my tail. I bet his Highness can't pull that stunt!"

Together, the three headed off into the shadowy thicket with their offerings in tow, eager for the All Hallows' Eve celebration to come.

THE LAST HALLOWEEN: AN ESSAY

In the little Tennessee town where I grew up, Halloween was for children. At the age of thirteen, you were pretty much expected to sit it out, hand out candy at the house with the old folks (your parents), or roll the principal's yard with two-ply Charmin. Now days, you can pretty much trick-or-treat until you're in your mid-twenties (freaky, but acceptable). Back in the late '60s and early '70s, you would be considered a "juvenile delinquent" if you showed up on someone's front porch with grease-painted face and one of your mother's spare pillowcases. The neighbors would be ready to call Joe Friday to come and haul you off to Juvie Hall.

My last real Halloween was in 1972... at least the last one that held all the privileges and benefits of childhood. As it drew near, I knew the end of something special was approaching and it saddened me. For as long as I could remember, Halloween had always been my favorite holiday. The smell of wood smoke in the air, the crunch of autumn leaves beneath the soles of your Red Ball sneakers, and the sense of adolescent community that the sight of dozens of Batmans (or is it *Batmen*?), ballerinas, and Frankenstein's Monsters roaming from house to house brought. That and the gradually increasing heaviness of your candy sack taking on loot at each lighted porch or concrete stoop. Yes, it was downright magical... but those who held the Power... the *adults*—the mayor, the school superintendent, the local churches—said it all ended after the big One-Two. The pleasures of trick-or-treating were off limits for those acne-ridden, voice-changing, awkward creatures known as the common teenager.

I knew, for quite some time, that this had been coming. All good things—at least good *childhood* things—must come to an end. First Santa Claus, then the Easter Bunny, then your precious Mr. Potato Heads and G.I. Joes. I was a fighter, though. I wanted to cling to childhood with fingernails anchored to the quick and teeth bared... especially where All Hallows' Eve was concerned. So, I decided I would do the last one up right. Pull out all the stops. Gather up enough candy to last me at least until I was twenty.

My brother Kevin and my cousin Donna also sensed my impending doom. Their beloved Ronald, the Lover of Monsters (and Dum-Dums and Bite-Size Snickers) was making a transition, albeit a forced one. At the beginning of October, we got together beneath the big magnolia tree in the back yard for a pow-wow.

"Won't you ever get to go trick-or-treating again?" Kevin asked me with a pout.

"No," I said grimly. "My time has come. Never again will I darken Old Lady Mangrum's door and hear her say 'Weren't you here an hour ago?' with her hair up in Coke can-sized curlers and a Marlboro Light dangling from her lower lip."

My confederates, ages eight and ten, still in their youthful prime, hung their heads in sorrow. Then we broke out the cherry Kool-Aid and vanilla wafers and partook of our final Halloween communion... and planned that season's festivities.

The following weekend we pooled our allowances and rode to town with our parents (for the entirety of our childhood, the city of Nashville was simply known as TOWN, at least to us rural rubes). We endured hair appointments and shoe shopping (a torture unto itself) and finally found ourselves in the hallowed halls of Grants Department Store. While our mothers went to check the prices of cake pans and foundation bras ('unmentionables', to young ears), we loudly invaded the Halloween section of the store.

Grants was the best place to do one's Halloween shopping. The manager must surely have been a child at heart, because it was always decorated with plastic pumpkins, glow-in-the-dark skeletons, and cardboard cutouts of cackling witches and arch-backed black cats that looked as though they had stuck their claws in a light socket. The candy aisle with its three-pound bags of suckers, bubble gum, and candy bars was always fully stocked, enticing us with the sugary bootie to come. But the best thing about Grants' Halloween section was the costumes. For the little kids there were costumes in colorful cardboard boxes with clear windows and the masks of monsters, astronauts, and hollow-eyed princesses staring blankly through. Folded underneath those disembodied faces were silk-screened body stockings of shimmering polyester; the type that would make an Eskimo sweat and were, thank God, patently FLAME-RETARDANT!

We weren't interested in the baby stuff, though. We were interested in something else entirely. Grants had a large wooden bin that was perhaps six feet long by four feet wide... filled nearly two feet deep with rubber masks. Every sort of goblin or ghoul, werewolf or devil, could be found in that treasure trove of limp and garishly-painted latex. They were substan-dard in workmanship by today's standards, but back then they were wonderfully creepy works of art. With total abandon (and ignoring our mothers' forewarnings of "Don't you DARE try on those germy things!"), we picked through the heap of leering, grinning, fang-bearing rubber, trying on each and every one. Thinking back, I can still smell that powdery latex odor; feel the disorienting, but delicious, claustrophobia of staring through sagging eyeholes at the muted brilliance of Grants overhead fluorescent lights, and the sensation of the elastic string cutting into the back of my head. For a moment, you were transformed. No longer human but belonging to a time-honored fraternity of the grisly and ghoulish, hunted by torch-wielding mobs and cross-bearing Van Helsings in the mountainous wilds of Transylvania.

After the hunting was over, our choices were made. Mine was a pale-faced, widow-peaked vampire, fangs dripping with blood. My brother chose a leering, red-faced devil... then changed his mind and picked a werewolf when I convinced him that our conservative, Christian mom would never allow him to walk the length and breadth of Sunnyfield Drive bearing the unholy countenance of Satan. Cousin Donna opted for a different approach, shunning the latex and going with one of those bizarre transparent masks that showed a hint of your true face, while adding the benefit of bushy black eyebrows and mustache, or bee-stung lips the color of fire-engine paint. She chose the Marilyn Monroe look and was certain that her mother would be more than happy to dye her hair platinum blond to complete the ensemble. Personally, I was doubtful that that would take place. My aunt Hazel was a bit more free-spirited than my mother, but I couldn't see her going down to the local Woolworths to buy a box of bleach-blond Clairol to fulfill a ten-year-old's Halloween fantasy.

We left Grants satisfied, with masks and a couple of life-sized glow skeletons (if you can call five-foot-tall life-sized) in hand. The first step of the planning and execution of my Last Halloween had been completed. But there was work still to come.

Before I was a writer, I was known as an artist. Ever since I had scrawled my first Fred Flintstone and Touché Turtle on my stand-up blackboard at the age of four, family and friends honored me with distinction of being "the little boy who could draw".

It was no exception that October. I was on fire with artistic inspiration. Many a sheet of wide-ruled notebook paper fell victim to pencil-drawn renderings of the Wolfman, the Mummy, and my favorite, the Creature from the Black Lagoon, as well as assorted bats, rats, cats, and spiders. Perhaps I saw this as my last-ditch effort to purge myself of every Halloween image imaginable and share them with my friends. After all, that time the following year, I would see no jolly jack-o'-lanterns or grinning skeletons upon my classroom wall. Instead there would be boring charts of the food group pyramid, the American presidents (from Washington to Nixon), and the cryptic Table of Elements.

One drawing I was particularly fond of that year was a profile of a withered man with one bulging eye, a rat-gnawed ear, and a protruding chin sporting three ingrown hairs. The coup de grâce was a large tenpenny nail that had been driven through the bridge of his crooked nose. I was particularly proud of that addition. I could imagine that the Lunch Lady had put it there with a ball-peen hammer for the crime of not finishing his green bean casserole... or that he had done the piercing himself—a sideshow geek who had mutilated his Durante-sized schnoz for the enjoyment of the paying crowd.

That drawing was the most popular of my Halloween gallery and, before long, every boy and girl in my seventh-grade class was requesting a copy to hang on their front door for Halloween night. Being the congenial and agreeable lad that I was, I readily agreed... but it was a daunting task. There were no office copiers in that day and age, only primitive mimeograph machines with royal-blue ink so toxic it would give a paper bag full of airplane model glue a solid run for its money. So, I set to work and hand-drew thirty-two of the one-eyed, nail-pierced geeks for my grinning classmates. Even the class bully wanted one. Inspired by his reign of terror, I added a word balloon hovering above the geek's snaggle-toothed mouth that pleaded "Here's my lunch money. Please don't hurt me!" The elementary school equivalent of Josef Mengele thought this was absolutely hilarious and so I was spared a purple nurple or an Indian rope burn (of my choice) for the following week.

After school, I would go home and continue the planning of my final trick-or-treating campaign. Since I was going as Count Dracula, I wanted my outfit to be as authentic as possible. I had no flowing black cape—there was none to be bought back then, to my knowledge—but my father did have a long, navy-blue overcoat that hung loosely and dangled past my knees, giving me sort of a Dark Shadows/Barnabas Collins look. I convinced my mother to let me wear my white Sunday shirt and necktie, but there would be no slacks or patent-leather shoes to complete the illusion of undeadness. This was a definite setback. Who would ever believe the dreaded Nosferatu would terrorize the countryside wearing blue jeans from the boys department at Sears and ratty basketball high-tops?

Weeks turned into days, days into hours, and soon Halloween came to the picturesque town of Pegram (population 705). The weatherman had predicted rain, but our prayers apparently reached the Big Guy's celestial ears and the storm clouds held their bladders until well after nine o'clock. It was a chilly evening, blustery, sending dead leaves skittering across the streets like an exodus of withered, brown spiders. Kevin, Donna, and I donned our alter-egos and prepared for the "festival of groveling and begging", as my curmudgeonly Grandpa Kelly called it. We had our costumes satisfactorily in place, Donna with a fancy silk scarf wrapped around her head rather than the hair-sprayed helmet of platinum-blond tresses she had formerly envisioned.

Mama was in the kitchen, preparing her largest mixing bowl and filling it with black and orange peanut butter kisses (the standard candy giveaway at the Kelly household). She mugged a mock expression of terror as we paraded past in our garb. We had no plastic pumpkins or Halloween-themed bags to carry with us, so we went to the cabinet beneath the sink where Mama kept her spare grocery bags. We found three good-sized Kroger bags and, appropriating scissors, cut oval handles in the opposing sides. There were no 'Pubics' grocery stores (as Aunt Wanda calls them) during that day and time, only Kroger, A&P, and good old reliable Piggly-Wiggly.

"Y'all be careful," Mama called to us as we started for the front door. Daddy sat in the living room, listening to George Jones on the big console stereo. He threw up his hand and grinned. We waved back and headed into the October night, the nasal tones of The Possum crooning "He Stopped Loving Her Today" drifting lazily behind us.

Now, you must understand, this was a different time. It was 1972. There was none of the fear of abductions and child molesters like there is today. Parents didn't follow their children around in cars and there was no such thing as trick-or-treating at the outlet mall or Trunk-or-Treat in the parking lot of the local church. Kids still had room to breathe and be kids, and one of the freedoms they enjoyed was venturing fearlessly into the night and trick-or-treating on their own.

I had secretly hoped for a full moon that evening, like any respectable vampire should, but if it was there, it was hidden behind a broad mat of dark clouds. We did our street first, going down one side, then back up the other. Although the temperature was hovering between the high 50s and low 60s, my rubber mask became sweltering. I began to sweat like a hog in a sauna and my frightening visage began to shift on me. I was leaving the McDowell house and heading across the yard, when the eyeholes of my vampire mask lost their alignment and, suddenly, I was as blind as a bat (no pun intended).

Suddenly, without warning, there was no ground beneath my feet. I took a spill and rolled into a drainage ditch. Fortunately, only my pride was hurt. I removed my mask and saw my brother and my cousin staring down at me.

"What are you doing in that ditch?" Kevin asked me.

"Remind me to pound you one when I get out!" I snapped.

There was one casualty to my fall in the ditch; my Kroger sack had split down the middle and the majority of the candy inside had scattered, like shrapnel from a detonated grenade. "Get your bottoms down in here and help me pick this stuff up," I told them. We didn't say 'ass' or even 'butt' back then; my mother said it was a 'vulgarity' and if she ever heard it cross our lips, we'd be walking the woods, picking our own switch.

Soon, we had the candy gathered and accounted for, bundled in the remains of the mangled bag. I couldn't help but moan when I saw that the next stop was Old Lady Mangrum's house. I slipped my mask back over my head, made sure the eyeholes were properly in place, and then we headed up the porch steps.

Old Lady Mangrum had no curlers in her hair that night, but the cigarette was there, as well as a suspicious look in her eyes. She examined my brother's costume closely. "Didn't I give you candy a half hour ago?" she asked. "I know I saw a dog like you come up here."

He was muffled, but I could hear the disdain in his voice. "I'm a werewolf."

When it was my turn, I held up my bag. "Do you have any Scotch tape?" I asked.

She told me to wait and then returned with a JCPenney shopping bag. It was big and roomy and would have held a bulldozer battery. "Thanks!" I said as I transferred my candy.

Maybe my luck was turning for the better. This was, without a doubt, the Cadillac of Halloween bags.

We ended up trick-or-treating across the entire town of Pegram, which is no mean feat, since it is scarcely a half mile from entrance to exit. We had no watch to tell the time, but we knew it was getting late. My last Halloween was slowly winding down.

Before we headed home, we decided to visit one more place. It was pretty ordinary—a ranch-style house with white brick and a big picture window in the front. There was a jack-o'-lantern on the porch and black and orange crepe paper draped from the banisters. Thinking it was a safe bet, we mounted the porch and knocked on the door.

A lady appeared—tall, skinny, with a beehive hairdo that had gone out of style with the Johnson Administration. She seemed excited to see us. "Come in, come in!" she urged. "I have something to show you!" Her enthusiasm was a little disturbing, but we went in anyway. I don't know why, but we did.

The living room was dimly lit and there were candles everywhere: on the end tables, the fireplace mantle, on the bar counter of the kitchenette nearby. "Come here!" the woman beckoned with a bony finger. "He wants to talk to you!"

Suddenly, a creepy feeling ran down my spine. *He? Who is he?*

Then we stepped farther into the living room and we knew. It was a man—a pretty overweight man, perhaps 300 pounds or more—sitting in a reclining chair, dressed in a wife-beater undershirt, flannel pajama pants, and bedroom slippers. But that wasn't the odd thing about him. His pudgy face was painted up like a clown and he wore a huge multi-colored wig on top of his head. He smiled lopsidedly at us and waved his hand. "Come here, kids!" he said, laughing sinisterly. "Come here… I have something to give you!"

Cautiously, we crept forward. We were scarcely four feet from the chair when I smelled the odor of beer and perspiration in the air. I saw a Budweiser can on an end table beside him. Looking around, I saw that there were several more sitting on the carpet beside his La-Z-Boy recliner.

"Open your bags!" he urged, still laughing. "Open 'em up and I'll give it to you!"

My brother stared at me with frightened eyes. I'd never seen a lycanthrope look so scared before.

Then the drunken guy in the clown makeup and the rainbow afro dropped foil-wrapped popcorn balls in our treat bags and said, "Happy Halloween!"

A few minutes later, we were outside and back on the street. We looked at each other and began to giggle... but there was more relief to our mirth than humor.

"That was so *weird!*" Donna said.

"You've got that right," I said. My heart was still pounding in my chest.

"What are we going to do with *these?*" Kevin asked, holding the crazy clown's popcorn ball in his hand.

We looked at one another, then tossed them in the nearest ditch and started home.

Halfway there, my brother turned to me. "So... you're not going trick-or-treating with us next year?"

"I can't dress up," I told him, "but I can walk with you."

He nodded quietly, then rummaged through his bag for a Bit-O-Honey.

Thinking back, I'm not sure if I ever did. The last Halloween I remember as a child, was the one we shared together in the fall of 1972.

These days I have three kids of my own. One has outgrown the joys and thrills of Halloween (having traded it in for a boyfriend, an iPhone, and an Xbox), while two still indulge in the same autumnal rituals I enjoyed as a child.

Things have changed now. Small-town Halloweens are similar to the ones I enjoyed, but they have an edge to them now, and a constant awareness that things are not always right in our world. I'm always a few steps behind them, making sure they don't step off the edge of a sidewalk, or that they don't stray too close to a patch of darkness between trees or shrubs. I reckon a parent has a right to be overly cautious in this day and time. There are dangers out there—dangers that were probably there when I was a kid, but not quite so apparent and identifiable.

But they have fun and, through the eyes of their masks and their infectious laughter, I relive the spirit of Halloweens past. Not as carefree and innocent as I once had it, but fun, nonetheless.

And if we end up with popcorn balls given away by demented clowns, we simply toss them in the nearest ditch and go our merry way.

MY TOP 10 FAVORITE HALLOWEEN STUFF OF THE '60S AND '70S!

Having grown up in the mid-1960s and early 1970s, Halloween seemed distinctly different than it does now. First, it was much more carefree and simplistic. Now days Mom and Dad have to follow you from street to street in the mini-van or even accompany you to the door of the neighbor's house to insure that no creepy pedophile nabs you, locks the door, and whisks you away to the basement. Either that, or you simply do Trunk-or-Treat at the local church parking lot, or do the candy thing, store to store, at some safe outlet mall. When I was a kid, we'd don our costumes, grab our T&T bags, and plunge head-long into the darkness, while our folks stayed behind to pass out treats to equally adventurous young'uns. And there was no DayGlo orange, glow sticks, or flashlights to distinguish us from the darkness. We were creatures of the night! We didn't want anyone to see us until we appeared at the glass of the storm door and heralded our arrival with a hearty "Trick-or-Treat!"

Also, kids these days don't seem to give Halloween a second thought until a day or two before the grand event. When I was a kid, we planned weeks, maybe *months*, ahead—indulging, scheming, soaking it all in in. Anticipating the coming of dusk on All Hallows' Eve and the delightfully spooky festivities that night would bring. In celebration of those bygone days of child-hoods past, I present to you my Top 10 Favorite Halloween Stuff of the '60s and '70s!

HALLOWEEN DECORATIONS

Back when I was a kid, we didn't have seven-foot blow-ups in the yard, synthetic spider webs, or zombie arms sprouting out of the autumn leaves (although that would have been cool!). Halloween decorations were much simpler. Of course, there was the traditional jack-o'-lantern to sit on the front porch. As for other decorations to embellish your "haunted house" you would usually go to your local Woolworths or five-and-dime store and get cardboard decorations to hang in your windows or on your walls. Witches, black cats, leering pumpkins, bats... the theme was pretty much set in stone, and there was the occasional Devil every now and then. But it was what graced your front door, to welcome hordes of trick-or-treaters, that mattered most. For our family it was the "Life-Sized Articulated Glow-in-the-Dark Skeleton". To tell the truth, it wasn't exactly "life-sized". It was usually only five feet tall... but if it had been anatomically scaled to my mother, who was four foot eleven and a half, then it would have been right on the money. The Glow Skeleton came in two different hues: bone yellow and ghoulish fluorescent green (my personal preference). My brother and I would usually pressure Dad into buying *two* skeletons—one for the front door and one for our bedroom door. Incidentally, my love of the Glow Skeleton later inspired me to write my Halloween short story, *Mister Glow-Bones* in my collection of Halloween stories and essays, *Mister Glow-Bones & Other Halloween Tales*.

HALLOWEEN COSTUMES IN A BOX

When you were a little kid in the '60s and '70s, more than likely the folks would buy you the tried-and-true Halloween Costume in a Box. This consisted of a hard-shell mask (with retaining elastic string) and a silk-screened jumpsuit of flame-retardant polyester. These costumes came in colorful boxes with a window in the front, usually with the hollow-eyed masks staring creepily at you from the other side. You could be anyone you wanted to be; cartoon characters, astronauts, superheroes, ballerinas, or your favorite monsters, be they generic (witches, ghosts, black cats) or of the Universal kind (Frankenstein's Monster, the Wolfman, the Creature). The majority of them were released by Ben Cooper, Inc., an American corporation based in Brooklyn, NY which manufactured Halloween costumes from the late 1930s to the late 1980s. I remember my favorite Costume in a Box at age 6 was Batman. The funny thing was, because of the wild success of the Batman TV series, the stores were selling Caped Crusader costumes to Batman-crazy boys months in advance. So, mine was well worn by the time Halloween rolled around (and to emulate Adam West—and to breathe a little easier), I had Mom cut away the lower half of the mask with her sewing scissors, leaving only the upper cowl to cover my youthful face.

HALLOWEEN MUSIC

If you grew up in the '60s and '70s, more than likely you listened to 78 rpm vinyl albums or 45 rpm singles on a little portable record player or your Dad's grown-up stereo in the living room. Our source of musical entertainment was the latter—a Sears Silvertone Console Stereo of Spanish design with burgundy-walled speakers on each side. Customarily, Dad played Merle Haggard, George Jones, or Buck Owens. As a child I remember lying in my bunkbed and hearing Johnny Cash walk the line on the opposite side of the bedroom wall. But around Halloween, Dad let us listen to our Halloween albums. Some were old classic radio show broadcasts like The Shadow or Orson Welles' The War of the Worlds, while others were spooky sound effects and goofy monster-themed songs like "Monster Mash" and "Purple People Eater". Our personal favorite was Disney's The Haunted Mansion album, sporting the fold-out dust jacket with the full-color story booklet stapled inside. I recall me, my brother, and my cousins lying in pitch darkness on the shag carpeting of the living room floor, giggling and shivering to the story of two children trapped within the mansion inhabited by 999 Happy Haunts. Incidentally, one of the kids was voiced by a pre-teen Ronnie Howard.

MONSTER MOVIES

When I was a kid, we didn't have DVDs or digital streaming like Netflix or Hulu. If you wanted to watch a monster movie—outside of going to the movie theater—you had two ways of doing it. You either stayed up late and watched the local creature feature (in the area I grew up in it was Sir Cecil Creepe on Nashville's Channel 4) or you begged your folks to buy you a cheap 8mm or Super 8 movie projector. I indulged in both, but buying your own little slices of horror cinema and manually threading them through the spools from reel to reel made it feel like big deal to a kid of nine or ten. You pretty much had two ways to watch them: the small reels (three and a half minutes) and big reels (fifteen minutes). Never mind that they were only snippets of the best scenes and had no sound whatsoever, they were just fun to own and watch. When we wanted our monster fix, we'd throw a blanket over the bedroom window and watch Godzilla stomp Tokyo or Frankenstein's Monster and the Wolfman battle it out on the bedroom wall.

RUBBER MONSTER MASKS

When you reached your preteen years, you normally wanted to ditch the Costumes in a Box and enter the big leagues. And that meant over-the-head rubber monster masks. There was just something about slipping the gaudy, gruesome second skins over your youthful head and breathing in that heady odor of latex rubber that told you that you had entered a higher realm of Halloween indulgence. Yes, you couldn't half see through the off-kilter eyeholes and you sweated like a sinner in church after only a few minutes, but to wear the leering visage of a hairy werewolf or a rotting zombie gave you a thrill that the children's hard-shell masks never could. Most of us hardcore monster enthusiasts yearned to own the big daddy of all horror disguises: the Don Post latex monster masks. We would gawk at that full-page advertisement in the back of Famous Monsters of Filmland magazine and dream of owning a full-head mask of the Creature from the Black Lagoon or the Wolfman or Mr.

Hyde. And, of course, if we ever managed to get the face masks, we would have to have the matching hands as well. Sadly, very few of us ever reached that level of monster mask ownership. At $39.99 per mask, it was a bit steep for a twelve-year-old's piddling allowance.

HORROR COMICS

When I was around ten or eleven, I started collecting comics. I always had a thing for Batman and the Flash and, when I got into Marvel, the Hulk and Spider-man were my favs. But from the beginning, I always bought the horror comics. I reckon it was my natural inclination toward the weird and macabre that drew me to comic books like DC's The House of Mystery, The Unexpected, and Swamp Thing, as well as Marvel's Werewolf by Night, Tomb of Dracula, and Man-Thing. I was too young to have enjoyed the ultra-bizarre (and "gasp" potentially immoral) tales of the EC Comics of the '50s, but, in a strange way, I still did. While my mom was pregnant with me in 1959, she came across a large stack of EC comics in the dusty attic of a house she was renting, while my Dad was serving in Korea and Germany. Throughout her pregnancy, she read horrifying tales of decaying corpses and flesh-eating monsters from such comics as Tales from the Crypt and The Vault of Horror, feeding me a steady diet of tantalizing terror as I floated in the darkness of the womb. You may say that had nothing to do with my inherent love of horror, but I beg to differ.

AURORA MONSTER MODELS

One of my favorite hobbies (around Halloween or otherwise) was assembling and painting Aurora monster models. It was always fun to head to the toy section of Sears (we bought everything at Sears back then), find your favorite monster in a box, then head back home and start bringing that plastic kit to life with airplane glue and those little glass jars of Testors model paint. I started my model-building in the early '70s, around the time Aurora released their glow-in-the dark line. I was always a stickler for detail, so I never used the glow heads or hands for the actual models, saving them for those little midget monsters you could build with the surplus parts you had left over. My favorites of the Aurora models were the Creature, King Kong, and Dr. Jekyll and Mr. Hyde, although the latter was of a much smaller scale than the others, along with the Witch. Aurora also put out Monster Scenes, which you could use to build your own mad scientist lab and torture chamber, featuring Dr. Deadly, the Frankenstein Monster, The Victim, and the scantily clad Vampirella.

GLOW FANGS, VAMPIRE BLOOD, & SCAR STUFF

Eventually, there would come the Halloween when you wanted to do some experimentation with your costume for that year. With me it was Count Dracula (I read the novel while in middle school and was completely obsessed with it!). Mirroring the dreaded Count (pun intended!) required some improvisation that a mere rubber mask couldn't pull off. So, I sojourned to the local Woolworths and acquired the traditional pair of glow-in-the-dark vampire fangs, as well as a tube of Vampire Blood and, for good measure, a tiny jar of Scar Stuff. Vampire Blood and Scar Stuff came out in the early '70s and, although they produced authentic appearing trickles of blood from the corners of your mouth and ghoulish scars and abrasions, they were a mom's nightmare around the Halloween season. It was nearly impossible to get Vampire Blood out of clothing and Scar Stuff (which basically had the consistency of flesh-colored snot) contained enough grease to stain clothes and furniture upholstery equally well.

MONSTER MAGAZINES

My number one source for a solid monster fix was undoubtedly Famous Monsters of Filmland magazine, edited by Forrest J. Ackerman (or simply "Uncle Forry" to us creature-loving kids). Uncle Forry possessed a tremendous love and appreciation for horror and science fiction cinema, one that extended from the silent era of The Phantom of the Opera and Metropolis, through

the '30s, '40s, and '50s heyday of the Universal Monster movies, and on into the '60s and '70s era of the Hammer horror
films, the Planet of the Apes phenomena , and even Star Wars.
I had the pleasure of actually meeting Uncle Forry at the first
World Horror Convention (he was hanging out in the monster
model room with none other than Robert "Psycho" Bloch) and
found my childhood hero to be both congenial and humble.
Other Warren Publishing magazines like Creepy, Eerie, and
Vampirella were on the newsstands for the taking, but unfortunately my mom prohibited me from partaking of them, claim-
ing that they were much too "adult" compared to my monthly
purchase of the latest Famous Monsters.

HALLOWEEN CANDY

And last, but certainly not least, there was the candy! The decorations, costumes, and activities may have embellished All
Hallows' Eve, but the hunting and procuring of sugary delights
was always the main objective. Whether we took a brown grocery bag Mom brought home from Kroger or A&P, or the sea-
sonal Brach's Candy trick-or-treat bags given away at the big
candy counter at—you guessed it—Sears, it was a requirement
to have a sturdy-enough receptacle to haul at least five pounds
of candy home in. Some kids toted those plastic pumpkins
around, but they filled up quickly and, by the time you'd done
two or three streets, it was like toting a heavy, orange bowling
ball around. When you got home, you would slip into your paja-
mas and dump that night's Halloween haul onto the kitchen
table or the living room carpet and begin the sorting process.
Miniature candy bars went into one pile (Snickers, Baby Ruth,
Almond Joys, Reese's cups, etc.), suckers and hard candy into
another, and the novelty items in a third (Razzles, Bottle Caps,
and the now politically incorrect candy cigarettes and bubble
gum cigars). Oh, and there was always a fourth pile of odd and
questionable treats that Mom had to inspect before giving the
okay or tossing them in the trash—things like popcorn balls,
apples, religious tracts, and even little tubes of toothpaste and
toothbrushes. Every now and then, we would be delighted to

find some pennies, dimes, or quarters in our bags, tossed there by some unprepared homeowner who had either run out of candy early or completely forgotten it was Halloween in the first place. But, sadly, those monetary treats were few and far between.

So, there you have it, Ol' Ron's top Halloween things of the '60s and '70s. These days I enjoy Halloween and trick-or-treating through my own kids, but I still cherish those fun, carefree days of preparing for and indulging in the most ghoulish holiday of the year.

ABOUT THE AUTHOR

Ronald Kelly was born November 20, 1959 in Nashville, Tennessee. He attended Pegram Elementary School and Cheatham County Central High School before starting his writing career.

Ronald Kelly began his writing career in 1986 and quickly sold his first short story, "Breakfast Serial," to *Terror Time Again* magazine. His first novel, *Hindsight* was released by Zebra Books in 1990. His audiobook collection, *Dark Dixie: Tales of Southern Horror*, was on the nominating ballot of the 1992 Grammy Awards for Best Spoken Word or Non-Musical Album. Zebra published eight of Ronald Kelly's novels from 1990 to 1996. Ronald's short fiction work has been published by *Cemetery Dance, Borderlands 3, Deathrealm, Dark at Heart, Hot Blood: Seeds of Fear*, and many more. After selling hundreds of thousands of books, the bottom dropped out of the horror market in 1996. So, when Zebra dropped their horror line in October 1996, Ronald Kelly stopped writing for almost ten years and worked various jobs including welder, factory worker, production manager, drugstore manager, and custodian.

In 2006, Ronald Kelly started writing again. In early 2008, Croatoan Publishing released his work *Flesh Welder* as a stand-alone chapbook, and it quickly sold out. In early 2009 Cemetery Dance Publications released a limited edition hardcover of his first short story collection, *Midnight Grinding & Other Twilight Terrors*. Also in 2010, Cemetery Dance released his first novel in over ten years called, *Hell Hollow* as a limited edition hardcover. Ronald's Zebra/Pinnacle horror novels were released by Thunderstorm Books as The Essential Ronald Kelly series. Each book contains a new novella related to the novel's original storyline. His eBooks and audiobooks are with Crossroad Press.

Ronald Kelly currently lives in a backwoods hollow in Brush Creek, Tennessee, with his wife, Joyce, and their three children.

Curious about other Crossroad Press books?
Stop by our site:
http://store.crossroadpress.com
We offer quality writing
in digital, audio, and print formats.

CPSIA information can be obtained
at www.ICGtesting.com
Printed in the USA
LVHW032335171220
674492LV00005B/286